The Marvellous Land of Oz

A SEQUEL TO
THE WIZARD OF OZ

by L. Frank Baum

Illustrations by John R. Neill

Armada

Also available in Armada

THE WIZARD OF OZ

First published in the U.S.A. about 1904.
First published in the U.K. in 1969 by
Wm. Collins Sons and Co. Ltd.
14 St. James's Place, London, S.W.1.
Third Impression November 1973

Printed in Great Britain
by Richard Clay (The Chaucer Press), Ltd.,
Bungay, Suffolk

Contents

1.

Tip Manufactures a Pumpkinhead

IN THE COUNTRY OF THE GILLIKINS, which is at the north of the Land of Oz, lived a youth called Tip. There was more to his name than that, for old Mombi often declared that his whole name was Tippetarius; but no one was expected to say such a long word when 'Tip' would do just as well.

This boy remembered nothing of his parents, for he had been brought when quite young to be reared by the old woman known as Mombi, whose reputation, I am sorry to say, was none of the best. For the Gillikin people had reason to suspect her of indulging in magical arts, and therefore hesitated to associate with her.

Mombi was not exactly a Witch, because the Good Witch who ruled that part of the Land of Oz had forbidden any other Witch to exist in her dominions. So Tip's guardian, however much she might aspire to working magic, realized it was unlawful to be more than a Sorceress, or at most a Wizardess.

Tip had to carry wood from the forest, so that the old woman might boil her pot. He also worked in the cornfields, hoeing and husking; and he fed the pigs and milked the four-horned cow that was Mombi's especial pride.

But you must not suppose he worked all the time, for he felt that would be bad for him. When sent to the forest, Tip often climbed trees for birds' eggs, or amused himself chasing the fleet white rabbits, or fishing in the brooks with bent pins. Then he would hastily gather his armful of wood and carry it home. And when he was supposed to be working in the cornfields, and the tall stalks hid him from Mombi's view, Tip would often dig in the gopher holes or—if the mood seized him—lie on his back between the rows of corn and take a nap. So, by taking care not to exhaust his strength, he grew as strong and rugged as a boy may be.

Mombi's curious magic often frightened her neighbours, and they treated her shyly, yet respectfully, because of her weird powers. But Tip frankly hated her, and took no pains to hide his feelings. Indeed, he sometimes showed less respect for the old woman than he should have done, considering she was his guardian.

There were pumpkins in Mombi's cornfields, lying golden red among the rows of green stalks; and these had been planted and carefully tended, so that the four-horned cow might eat them in the wintertime. But one day, after the corn had all been cut and stacked, and Tip was carrying the pumpkins to the stable, he took a notion to make a jack-o'-lantern and try to give the old woman a fright with it.

So he selected a fine, big pumpkin—one with a lustrous, orange-red colour—and began carving it. With the point of his knife he made two round eyes, a three-cornered nose, and a mouth shaped like a new moon. The face, when completed, could not have been considered strictly beautiful; but it wore a smile so big and broad, and was so jolly in expression, that even Tip laughed as he looked admiringly at his work.

The child had no playmates, so he did not know that boys often dig out the inside of a pumpkin jack, and in the space thus made put a lighted candle to make the face more startling; but he conceived an idea of his own that promised to be quite as effective. He decided to manufacture the form of a man, who would wear this pumpkin head, and to stand it in a place where old Mombi would meet it face to face.

'And then,' said Tip to himself, with a laugh, 'she'll squeal louder than the brown pig does when I pull her tail, and shiver with fright worse than I did last year when I had the ague!'

He had plenty of time to accomplish this task, for Mombi had gone to a village—to buy groceries, she said—and it was a journey of at least two days.

So he took his axe to the forest and selected some stout, straight saplings, which he cut down and trimmed of all their twigs and leaves. From these he would make the arms and legs and feet of his man. For the body, he stripped a sheet of thick bark from around a big tree, and with much labour fashioned it into a cylinder of about the right size, pinning the edges together with wooden pegs. Then, whistling happily as he worked, he carefully jointed the limbs and fastened them to the body with pegs whittled into shape with his knife.

By the time this feat had been accomplished, it began to grow dark, and Tip remembered he must milk the cow and feed the pigs. So he picked up his wooden man and carried it back to the house with him.

During the evening, by the light of the fire in the kitchen, Tip carefully rounded all the edges of the joints and smoothed the rough places in a neat and workmanlike manner. Then he stood the figure up against the wall and admired it. It seemed remarkably tall, even for a full-grown man; but that was a good point in a small boy's eyes, and Tip did not object at all to the size of his creation.

Next morning, when he looked at his work again, Tip saw he had forgotten to give the dummy a neck, by means of which he might fasten the pumpkin head to the body. So he went again to the forest, which was not far away, and chopped from a tree several pieces of wood with which to complete his work. When he returned he fastened a cross-piece to the upper end of the body, making a hole through the centre to hold the neck upright. The bit of wood which formed this neck was also sharpened at the upper end, and when all was ready Tip put on the pumpkin head, pressing it well down on to the neck, and found that it fitted very well. The head could be turned to one side or the other, as he pleased, and the hinges of the arms and legs allowed him to place the dummy in any position he desired.

'Now, that,' declared Tip proudly, 'is really a very fine man, and it ought to frighten several screeches out of old Mombi! But it would be much more life-like if it were properly dressed.'

To find clothing proved no easy task; but Tip boldly ransacked the great chest in which Mombi kept all her keepsakes and treasures, and at the very bottom he discovered some purple trousers, a red shirt, and a pink waistcoat which was dotted with white spots. These he carried away to his man and succeeded, although the garments did not fit very well, in dressing the creature in a jaunty fashion. Some knit stockings belonging to Mombi and a much-worn pair of his own shoes completed the man's apparel, and Tip was so delighted that he laughed aloud.

'I must give him a name!' he cried. 'So good a man as this must surely have a name. I believe,' he added, after a moment's thought, 'I will name the fellow Jack Pumpkinhead!'

2.

The Marvellous Powder of Life

AFTER CONSIDERING THE MATTER CAREFULLY, Tip decided
that the best place to locate Jack would be at the bend in
the road, a little way from the house. So he started to carry
his man there, but found him heavy and rather awkward to
handle. After dragging the creature a short distance, Tip
stood him on his feet; and by first bending the joints of
one leg and then those of the other, at the same time pushing from behind, the boy managed to induce Jack to walk
to the bend in the road. It was not accomplished without
a few tumbles, and Tip really worked harder than he ever
had in the fields or forest; but a love of mischief urged him
on, and it pleased him to test the cleverness of his work-
manship.

'Jack's all right, and works fine!' he said to himself,
panting with the unusual exertion. But just then he discovered the man's left arm had fallen off in the journey;
so he went back to find it, and afterwards, by whittling a
new and stouter pin for the shoulder joint, he repaired
the injury so successfully that the arm was stronger than
before. Tip also noticed that Jack's pumpkin head had

twisted around until he faced his back, but this was easily remedied. When at last the man was set up facing the turn in the path where old Mombi was to appear, he looked natural enough to be a fair imitation of a Gillikin farmer—and strange enough to startle anyone coming on him unawares.

As it was yet too early in the day to expect the old woman to return home, Tip went down into the valley below the farmhouse and began to gather nuts from the trees that grew there.

However, old Mombi returned earlier than usual. She had met a crooked Wizard who resided in a lonely cave in the mountains, and had traded several important secrets of magic with him. Having in this way secured three new recipes, four magical powders, and a selection of herbs of wonderful power and potency, she hobbled home as fast as she could, in order to test her new sorceries.

So intent was Mombi on the treasures she had gained that when she turned the bend in the road and caught a glimpse of the man she merely nodded and said, 'Good evening, sir.'

But a moment after, noting that the person did not move or reply, she cast a shrewd glance into his face and discovered his pumpkin head, elaborately carved by Tip's jack-knife.

'Heh!' ejaculated Mombi, giving a sort of grunt; 'that rascally boy has been playing tricks again! Very good! ve—ry *good*! I'll beat him black and blue for trying to scare me in this fashion!'

Angrily, she raised her stick to smash in the grinning

pumpkin head of the dummy; but a sudden thought made her pause, the uplifted stick left motionless in the air.

'Why, here is a good chance to try my new powder!' said she eagerly. 'And then I can tell whether that crooked Wizard has fairly traded secrets, or whether he fooled me as wickedly as I fooled him.'

So she set down her basket and began fumbling in it for one of the precious powders she had obtained.

While Mombi was thus occupied, Tip strolled back, with his pockets full of nuts, and discovered the old woman standing beside his man and apparently not the least bit frightened by it.

At first he was greatly disappointed, but the next moment he became curious to know what Mombi was going to do. So he hid behind a hedge, where he could see without being seen, and watched.

After some search, the woman drew from her basket an old pepper-box, upon the faded label of which the Wizard had written with a lead pencil: 'Powder of Life.'

'Ah—here it is!' she cried joyfully. 'And now let us see if it is potent. The stingy Wizard didn't give me much of it, but I guess there's enough for two or three doses.'

Tip was much surprised when he overheard this speech. Then he saw old Mombi raise her arm and sprinkle the powder from the box over the pumpkin head of his man Jack. She did this in the same way one would pepper a baked potato, and the powder sifted down from Jack's head and scattered over the red shirt and pink waistcoat and purple trousers Tip had dressed him in, and a portion even fell upon the patched and worn shoes.

Then, putting the pepper-box back into the basket, Mombi lifted her left hand, with its little finger pointed upward, and said, '*Weaugh!*'

Then she lifted her right hand, with the thumb pointed upward, and said, '*Teaugh!*'

Then she lifted both hands, with all the fingers and thumbs spread out, and cried, '*Peaugh!*'

Jack Pumpkinhead stepped back a pace at this, and said in a reproachful voice, 'Don't yell like that! Do you think I'm deaf?'

Old Mombi danced around him, frantic with delight. 'He lives!' she screamed. 'He lives!—he lives!'

Then she threw her stick into the air and caught it as it came down; and she hugged herself with both arms and tried to do a step of a jig, and all the time she repeated rapturously, 'He lives!—he lives!'

Now you may well suppose that Tip observed all this with amazement.

At first he was so frightened and horrified that he wanted to run away, but his legs trembled and shook so badly that he couldn't. Then it struck him as a very funny thing for Jack to come to life, especially as the expression on his pumpkin face was so droll and comical it excited laughter on the instant. So, recovering from his first fear, Tip began to laugh; and the merry peals reached old Mombi's ears and made her hobble quickly to the hedge, where she seized Tip's collar and dragged him back to where she had left her basket and the pumpkin-headed man.

'You naughty, sneaking, wicked boy!' she exclaimed, furiously; 'I'll teach you to spy out my secrets and to make fun of me!'

'I wasn't making fun of you,' protested Tip. 'I was laughing at old Pumpkinhead! Look at him! Isn't he a picture, though?'

'I hope you are not reflecting on my personal appearance,' said Jack; and it was so funny to hear his grave voice, while his face continued to wear its jolly smile, that Tip again burst into laughter.

Even Mombi was not without a curious interest in the man her magic had brought to life, for after staring at him intently she asked, 'What do you know?'

'Well, that is hard to tell,' replied Jack. 'For although I feel that I know a tremendous lot, I am not yet aware how much there is in the world to find out about. It will take me a little time to discover whether I am very wise or very foolish.'

'To be sure,' said Mombi thoughtfully.

'But what are you going to do with him, now he is alive?' asked Tip, wondering.

'I must think it over,' answered Mombi. 'But we must get home at once, for it is growing dark. Help the Pumpkinhead to walk.'

'Never mind me,' said Jack; 'I can walk as well as you can. Haven't I got legs and feet, and aren't they jointed?'

'Are they?' asked the woman, turning to Tip.

'Of course they are; I made 'em myself,' returned the boy with pride.

So they started for the house; but when they reached the farmyard old Mombi led the pumpkin man to the cow

stable and shut him up in an empty stall, fastening the door securely on the outside.

'I've got to attend to you, first,' she said to Tip.

Hearing this, the boy became uneasy; for he knew Mombi had a bad and revengeful heart, and would not hesitate to do any evil thing.

They entered the house. It was a round, dome-shaped structure, as are nearly all the farmhouses in the Land of Oz.

Mombi bade the boy light a candle, while she put her basket in a cupboard and hung her cloak on a peg. Tip obeyed quickly, for he was afraid of her.

After the candle had been lighted, Mombi ordered him to build a fire in the hearth, and while Tip was thus engaged the old woman ate her supper. When the flames began to crackle, the boy came to her and asked for some bread and cheese; but Mombi refused.

'I'm hungry!' said Tip, in a sulky tone.

'You won't be hungry long,' replied Mombi with a grim look.

The boy didn't like this speech, for it sounded like a threat; but he happened to remember he had nuts in his pocket, so he cracked some of those and ate them while the woman rose, shook the crumbs from her apron, and hung above the fire a small black kettle.

Then she measured out equal parts of milk and vinegar and poured them into the kettle. Next she produced several packets of herbs and powders, and began adding a portion of each to the contents of the kettle. Occasionally she would draw near the candle and read from a yellow paper the recipe of the mess she was concocting.

As Tip watched her his uneasiness increased.

'What is that for?' he asked.

'For you,' returned Mombi briefly.

Tip wriggled around upon his stool and stared a while at the kettle, which was beginning to bubble. Then he would glance at the stern and wrinkled features of the Witch. He wished he were any place but in that dim and smoky kitchen, where even the shadows cast by the candle upon the wall were enough to give one the horrors. So an hour passed away, during which the silence was broken only by the bubbling of the pot and the hissing of the flames.

Finally Tip spoke again.

'Have I got to drink that stuff?' he asked, nodding towards the pot.

'Yes,' said Mombi.

'What'll it do to me?' asked Tip.

'If it's properly made,' replied Mombi, 'it will change or transform you into a marble statue.'

Tip groaned, and wiped the perspiration from his forehead with his sleeve.

'I don't want to be a marble statue!' he protested.

'That doesn't matter; I want you to be one,' said the old woman, looking at him severely.

'What use'll I be then?' asked Tip. 'There won't be anyone to work for you.'

'I'll make the Pumpkinhead work,' said Mombi.

'Why don't you change me into a goat, or a chicken?' Tip asked anxiously. 'You can't do anything with a marble statue.'

'Oh, yes, I can,' returned Mombi. 'I'm going to plant a flower garden next spring, and I'll put you in the middle of it, for an ornament. I wonder I haven't thought of that before; you've been a bother to me for years.'

At this terrible speech, Tip felt the beads of perspiration starting all over his body; but he sat still and shivered and looked anxiously at the kettle.

'Perhaps it won't work,' he muttered, in a voice that sounded weak and discouraged.

'Oh, I think it will,' answered Mombi cheerfully. 'I

seldom make a mistake.'

Again there was a period of silence—a silence so long and gloomy that when Mombi finally lifted the kettle from the fire it was close to midnight.

'You cannot drink it until it has become quite cold,' announced the old Witch—for in spite of the law, she had acknowledged practising witchcraft. 'We must both go to bed now, and at daybreak I will call you and at once complete your transformation into a marble statue.'

With this she hobbled into her room, bearing the steaming kettle with her, and Tip heard her close and lock the door.

The boy did not go to bed as he had been commanded to do, but still sat glaring at the embers of the dying fire.

3.
The Flight of the Fugitives

'IT'S A HARD THING to be a marble statue,' Tip thought rebelliously, 'and I'm not going to stand it. For years I've been a bother to her, she says; so she's going to get rid of me. Well, there's an easier way than to become a statue. No boy could have any fun for ever standing in the middle of a flower garden; I'll run away, that's what I'll do—and I'll go before she makes me drink that nasty stuff in the kettle.'

He waited until the snores of the old Witch announced she was fast asleep, and then he arose softly and went to the cupboard to find something to eat. No use starting on a journey without food.

He found some crusts of bread, but he had to look into Mombi's basket to find the cheese she had brought from the village. While turning over the contents of the basket, he came upon the pepper-box which contained the Powder of Life.

'I may as well take this with me,' he thought, 'or Mombi'll be using it to make more mischief with.' So he put the box in his pocket, together with the bread and cheese.

Then he cautiously left the house and latched the door behind him. Outside, both moon and stars shone brightly, and the night seemed peaceful and inviting after the close and ill-smelling kitchen.

'I'll be glad to get away,' said Tip softly, 'for I never did like that old woman. I wonder how I ever came to live with her.'

He was walking slowly towards the road when a thought made him pause.

'I don't like to leave Jack Pumpkinhead to the tender mercies of old Mombi,' he muttered. 'And Jack belongs to me, for I made him—even if the old Witch did bring him to life.'

He retraced his steps to the cow stable and opened the door of the stall where the pumpkin-headed man had been left.

Jack was standing in the middle of the stall, and by the moonlight Tip could see he was smiling just as jovially as ever.

'Come on!' said the boy, beckoning

'Where to?' asked Jack.

'You'll know as soon as I do,' answered Tip, smiling sympathetically into the pumpkin face. 'All we've got to do now is to tramp.'

'Very well,' returned Jack, and walked awkwardly out of the stable and into the moonlight.

Tip turned towards the road, and the man followed him. Jack walked with a sort of limp, and occasionally one of the joints of his legs would turn backward, instead of frontwise, almost causing him to tumble. But the Pumpkinhead was quick to notice this, and began to take more pains to step carefully.

Tip led him along the path without stopping an instant. They could not go very fast, but they walked steadily; and by the time the moon sank away and the sun peeped over the hills they had travelled so great a distance that the boy had no reason to fear pursuit from the old Witch. Moreover, he had turned first into one path and then into another, so anyone trying to follow them would find it very difficult.

Fairly satisfied that he had escaped—for a time at least —being turned into a marble statue, the boy stopped his companion and seated himself on a rock.

'Let's have some breakfast,' he said.

Jack Pumpkinhead watched Tip curiously, but refused to join in the repast.

'I don't seem to be made the same way you are,' he said.

'I know you are not,' returned Tip; 'for I made you.'

'Oh! Did you?' asked Jack.

'Certainly. And put you together. And carved your eyes and nose and ears and mouth,' said Tip proudly. 'And dressed you.'

Jack looked at his body and limbs critically.

'It strikes me you made a very good job of it,' he remarked.

'Just so-so,' replied Tip modestly, for he began to see certain defects in the construction of his man. 'If I'd known we were going to travel together I might have been a little more particular.'

'Why, then,' said the Pumpkinhead, in a tone that expressed surprise, 'you must be my creator—my parent—my father!'

'Or your inventor,' replied the boy with a laugh. 'Yes, my son; I really believe I am!'

'Then I owe you obedience,' continued the man, 'and you owe me—support.'

'That's it exactly,' declared Tip, jumping up. 'So let us be off.'

'Where are we going?' asked Jack, when they had resumed their journey.

'I'm not exactly sure,' said the boy, 'but I believe we are headed south, and that will bring us, sooner or later, to the Emerald City.'

'What city is that?' inquired the Pumpkinhead.

'Why, it's the centre of the Land of Oz, and the biggest town in all the country. I've never been there myself, but I've heard all about its history. It was built by a mighty and wonderful Wizard named Oz, and everything there is of a green colour—just as everything in this Country of the Gillikins is purple.'

'Is everything here purple?' asked Jack.

'Of course it is. Can't you see?' returned the boy.

'I believe I must be colour blind,' said the Pumpkin-head, after staring about him.

'Well, the grass is purple, and the trees are purple, and the houses and fences are purple,' explained Tip. 'Even the mud in the roads is purple. But in the Emerald City everything is green that is purple here. And in the Country of the Munchkins, over at the East, everything is blue; and in the South Country of the Quadlings everything is red; and in the West Country of the Winkies, where the Tin Woodman rules, everything is yellow.'

'Oh!' said Jack. Then, after a pause, he asked: 'Did you say a Tin Woodman rules the Winkies?'

'Yes; he was one of those who helped Dorothy to destroy the Wicked Witch of the West, and the Winkies were so grateful that they invited him to become their ruler—just as the people of the Emerald City invited the Scarecrow to rule them.'

'Dear me!' said Jack. 'I'm getting confused with all this history. Who is the Scarecrow?'

'Another friend of Dorothy's,' replied Tip.

'And who is Dorothy?'

'She was a girl that came here from Kansas, a place in the big outside world. She got blown to the Land of Oz by a cyclone, and while she was here the Scarecrow and the Tin Woodman accompanied her on her travels.'

'And where is she now?'

'Glinda the Good, who rules the Quadlings, sent her

home again,' said the boy.

'Oh. And what became of the Scarecrow?'

'I told you. He rules the Emerald City,' answered Tip.

'I thought you said it was ruled by a wonderful Wizard,' objected Jack, seeming more and more confused.

'Well, so I did. Now, pay attention, and I'll explain it,' said Tip, speaking slowly and looking the smiling Pumpkinhead squarely in the eye. 'Dorothy went to the Emerald City to ask the Wizard to send her back to Kansas; and the Scarecrow and the Tin Woodman went with her. But the Wizard couldn't send her back, because he wasn't as much of a Wizard as he might have been. And then they got angry at the Wizard, and threatened to expose him; so the Wizard made a big balloon and escaped in it, and no one has ever seen him since.'

'Now, that is very interesting history,' said Jack, well pleased; 'and I understand it perfectly—all but the explanation.'

'I'm glad you do,' responded Tip. 'After the Wizard was gone, the people of the Emerald City made His Majesty the Scarecrow, their King; and I have heard that he became a very popular ruler.'

'Are we going to see this queer King?' asked Jack, with interest.

'I think we may as well,' replied the boy; 'unless you have something better to do.'

'Oh, no, dear Father,' said the Pumpkinhead. 'I am quite willing to go wherever you please.'

4.

Tip Makes an Experiment in Magic

THE BOY, small and rather delicate in appearance, was somewhat embarrassed at being called 'Father' by the tall, awkward, pumpkin-headed man; but to deny the relationship would involve another long and tedious explanation, so he changed the subject by asking, abruptly:

'Are you tired?'

'Of course not!' replied the other. 'But,' he continued, after a pause, 'it is quite certain I shall wear out my wooden joints if I keep on walking.'

Tip reflected, as they journeyed on, that this was true. He began to regret that he had not constructed the wooden limbs more carefully and substantially. Yet how could he ever have guessed that the man he had made merely to scare old Mombi with would be brought to life by means of a magical powder contained in an old pepper-box?

So he ceased to reproach himself, and began to think how he might improve on Jack's weak joints.

While thus engaged they came to the edge of a wood, and the boy sat down on an old sawhorse that some woodcutter had left there, to rest.

'Why don't you sit down?' he asked the Pumpkinhead.

'Won't it strain my joints?' inquired the other.

'Of course not. It'll rest them,' declared the boy.

So Jack tried to sit down; but as soon as he bent his joints farther than usual they gave way altogether, and he came clattering to the ground with such a crash that Tip feared he was entirely ruined.

He rushed to the man, lifted him to his feet, straightened his arms and legs, and felt of his head to see if by chance it had become cracked. But Jack seemed to be in pretty good shape after all, and Tip said to him:

'I guess you'd better remain standing. It seems the safest way.'

'Very well, dear Father; just as you say,' replied the smiling Jack, who had been in no wise confused by his tumble.

Tip sat down again. Presently the Pumpkinhead asked:

'What is that thing you are sitting on?'

'Oh, this is a horse,' replied the boy, carelessly.

'What is a horse?' demanded Jack.

'A horse? Why, there are two kinds of horses,' returned Tip, slightly puzzled how to explain. 'One kind of horse is alive, and has four legs and a head and a tail. And people ride on its back.'

'I understand,' said Jack, cheerfully. 'That's the kind of horse you are now sitting on.'

'No, it isn't,' answered Tip, promptly.

'Why not? That one has four legs, and a head, and a tail.'

Tip looked at the sawhorse more carefully, and found

that the Pumpkinhead was right. The body had been formed from a tree trunk, and a branch had been left sticking up at one end that looked very much like a tail. In the other end were two big knots that resembled eyes, and a place had been chopped away that might easily be mistaken for the horse's mouth. As for the legs, they were four straight limbs cut from trees and stuck fast into the body, being spread wide apart so that the sawhorse would stand firmly when a log was laid across it to be sawed.

'This thing resembles a real horse more than I imagined,' said Tip, trying to explain. 'But a real horse is alive, and trots and prances and eats oats; while this is nothing more than a sawhorse, made of wood, and used to saw logs upon.'

'If it were alive, wouldn't it trot and prance and eat oats?' inquired the Pumpkinhead.

'It would trot and prance perhaps, but it wouldn't eat oats,' replied the boy, laughing at the idea. 'And of course it can't ever be *really* alive, because it's wood.'

'So am I,' answered the man.

Tip looked at him in surprise.

'Why, so you are!' he exclaimed. 'And the magic powder that brought you to life is here in my pocket.'

He brought out the pepper-box and eyed it curiously.

'I wonder,' said he musingly, 'if it would bring the saw-horse to life.'

'If it would,' returned Jack calmly, for nothing seemed to surprise him, 'I could ride on its back, and that would save my joints from wearing out.'

'I'll try it!' cried the boy, jumping up. 'But I wonder if

I can remember the words old Mombi said, and the way she held her hands up.'

He thought it over for a minute. He had watched carefully from the hedge, had seen every motion of the old Witch and listened to her words, and believed he could repeat exactly what she had said and done.

So he began by sprinkling some of the magic Powder of Life from the pepper-box on the body of the sawhorse. Then he lifted his left hand, with the little finger pointing upward, and said, '*Weaugh!*'

'What does that mean, dear Father?' asked Jack, curiously.

'I don't know,' answered Tip. Then he lifted his right hand, with the thumb pointing upward, and said, '*Teaugh!*'

'What's that, dear Father?' inquired Jack.

'It means you must keep quiet!' replied the boy, provoked at being interrupted at this moment.

'How fast I am learning!' remarked the Pumpkinhead, with his eternal smile.

Tip now lifted both hands above his head, with all the fingers and thumbs spread out, and cried in a loud voice, '*Peaugh!*'

Immediately the sawhorse moved, stretched its legs, yawned with its chopped-out mouth, and shook a few grains of the powder off its back. The rest of the powder seemed to have vanished into the body of the horse.

'Good!' called Jack, while the boy looked on in astonishmen. 'You are a very clever Sorcerer, dear Father!'

5.

The Awakening of the Sawhorse

THE SAWHORSE, finding himself alive, seemed even more astonished than Tip. He rolled his knotty eyes from side to side, taking a first wondering view of the world in which he now had so important an existence. Then he tried to look at himself; but he had indeed no neck to turn, so that in the endeavour to see his body he kept circling around and around, without catching even a glimpse of it. His legs were stiff and awkward, for there were no knee joints in them, so that presently he bumped against Jack Pumpkinhead and sent him tumbling on the moss that lined the road.

Tip became alarmed at this accident, as well as at the persistence of the Sawhorse in prancing around in a circle, so he called out : 'Whoa! Whoa, there!'

The Sawhorse paid no attention whatever to this comband and the next instant brought one of his wooden legs down upon Tip's foot so forcibly that the boy danced away in pain to a safer distance, from where he again yelled : 'Whoa! Whoa, I say!'

Jack had now managed to raise himself to a sitting position, and he looked at the Sawhorse with much interest.

'I don't believe the animal can hear you,' he remarked.

'I shout loud enough, don't I?' asked Tip.

'Yes; but the horse has no ears,' said the smiling Pumpkinhead.

'Sure enough!' exclaimed Tip, noting the fact for the first time. 'How, then, am I going to stop him?'

But at that instant the Sawhorse stopped himself, having concluded it was impossible to see his own body. He saw Tip, however, and came close to the boy to observe him more fully.

It was really comical to see the creature walk; for it moved the legs on its right side together, and those on its left side together, as a pacing horse does; and that made its body rock sidewise, like a cradle.

Tip patted it upon the head, and said, 'Good boy! Good boy!' in a coaxing tone; and the Sawhorse pranced away to examine with its bulging eyes the form of Jack Pump-kinhead.

'I must find a halter for him,' said Tip; and having made a search in his pocket, he produced a roll of strong cord. Unwinding this, he approached the Sawhorse and tied the cord around its neck, afterwards fastening the other end to a large tree. The Sawhorse, not understanding the action, stepped backward and snapped the string easily; but it made no attempt to run away.

'He's stronger than I thought,' said the boy, 'and rather obstinate, too.'

'Why don't you make him some ears?' asked Jack. 'Then you can tell him what to do.'

'That's a splendid idea!' said Tip. 'How did you happen to think of it?'

'Why, I didn't think of it,' answered the Pumpkinhead; 'I didn't need to, for it's the simplest and easiest thing to do.'

So Tip got out his knife and fashioned some ears out of the bark of a small tree.

'I mustn't make them too big,' he said, as he whittled, 'or our horse would become a donkey.'

'How is that?' inquired Jack, from the roadside.

'Why, a horse has bigger ears than a man, and a donkey has bigger ears than a horse,' explained Tip.

'Then, if my ears were longer, would I be a horse?' asked Jack,

'My friend,' said Tip gravely, you'll never be anything but a Pumpkinhead, no matter how big your ears are.'

'Oh,' returned Jack, nodding; 'I think I understand.'

'If you do, you're a wonder,' remarked the boy; 'but there's no harm in *thinking* you understand. I guess these ears are ready now. Will you hold the horse while I stick them on?'

'Certainly, if you'll help me up,' said Jack.

So Tip raised him to his feet, and the Pumpkinhead went to the horse and held its head while the boy bored two holes in it with the knife blade and inserted the ears.

'They make him look very handsome,' said Jack admiringly.

But those words, spoken close to the Sawhorse, and being the first sounds the animal had ever heard, so startled him that he made a bound forward and tumbled Tip on one side and Jack on the other. Then he continued to rush forward as if frightened by the clatter of his own footsteps.

'Whoa!' shouted Tip, picking himself up; 'whoa! you idiot—whoa!'

The Sawhorse would probably have paid no attention to this, but just then its leg went into a gopher hole and it stumbled head over heels to the ground, where it lay upon its back, frantically waving its four legs in the air.

Tip ran up to it.

'You're a nice sort of a horse, I must say!' he exclaimed. 'Why didn't you stop when I yelled "whoa"?'

'Does "whoa" mean to stop?' asked the Sawhorse, in a surprised voice, as it rolled its eyes upward to look at the boy.

'Of course it does,' answered Tip.

'And a hole in the ground means to stop, also, doesn't it?' continued the horse.

'To be sure—unless you step over it,' said Tip.

'What a strange place this is,' the creature exclaimed, as if amazed. 'What am I doing here, anyway?'

'Why, I've brought you to life,' answered the boy; 'but it won't hurt you any, if you mind me and do as I tell you.'

'Then I will do as you tell me,' replied the Sawhorse humbly. 'But what happened to me a moment ago? I don't seem to be just right, someway.'

'You're upside down,' explained Tip. 'But just keep those legs still a minute and I'll set you right side up again.'

'How many sides have I?' asked the creature, wonderingly.

'Several,' said Tip, briefly. 'But do keep those legs still.'

The Sawhorse now became quiet, and held his legs rigid; so that Tip, after several efforts, was able to roll him over and set him upright.

'Ah, I seem all right now,' said the queer animal, with a sigh.

'One of your ears is broken,' Tip announced, after a careful examination. 'I'll have to make a new one.'

Then he led the Sawhorse back to where Jack was vainly struggling to regain his feet, and after assisting the Pumpkinhead to stand upright, Tip whittled out a new ear and fastened it to the horse's head.

'Now,' said he, addressing his steed, 'pay attention to what I'm going to tell you. "Whoa!" means to stop; "get-up!" means to walk forward; "trot!" means to go as fast as you can. Understand?'

'I believe I do,' returned the horse.

'Very good. We are all going on a journey to the Emerald City, to see His Majesty the Scarecrow; and Jack Pumpkinhead is going to ride on your back, so he won't wear out his joints.'

'I don't mind,' said the Sawhorse. 'Anything that suits you suits me.'

Then Tip assisted Jack to get on the horse.

'Hold on tight,' he cautioned, 'or you may fall off and crack your pumpkinhead.'

'That would be horrible!' said Jack, with a shudder. 'What shall I hold on to?'

'Why, hold on to his ears,' replied Tip, after a moment's hesitation.

'Don't do that!' remonstrated the Sawhorse; 'for then I can't hear.'

That seemed reasonable, so Tip tried to think of something else.

'I'll fix it!' said he, at length. He went into the wood and cut a short length of limb from a young, stout tree. One end of this he sharpened to a point, and then he dug a hole in the back of the Sawhorse, just behind its head. Next he brought a piece of rock from the road and hammered the post firmly into the animal's back.

'Stop! Stop!' shouted the horse. 'You're jarring me terribly.'

'Does it hurt?' asked the boy.

'Not exactly hurt,' answered the animal, 'but it makes me quite nervous to be jarred.'

'Well, it's all over now,' said Tip encouragingly. 'Now,

Jack, be sure to hold fast to this post, and then you can't fall off and get smashed.'

So Jack held on tight, and Tip said to the horse, 'Get-up.'

The obedient creature at once walked forward, rocking from side to side as he raised his feet from the ground.

Tip walked beside the Sawhorse, quite content with this addition to their party. Presently he began to whistle.

'What does that sound mean?' asked the horse.

'Don't pay any attention to it,' said Tip. 'I'm just whistling; that only means I'm pretty well satisfied.'

'I'd whistle myself, if I could push my lips together,' remarked Jack. 'I fear, dear Father, that in some respects I am sadly lacking.'

After journeying on for some distance, the narrow path they were following turned into a broad roadway, paved with yellow brick. By the side of the road Tip noticed a signpost that read:

NINE MILES TO THE EMERALD CITY

But it was now growing dark, so he decided to camp for the night by the roadside and to resume the journey next morning by daybreak. He led the Sawhorse to a grassy mound upon which grew several bushy trees, and carefully assisted the Pumpkinhead to alight.

'I think I'll lay you upon the ground overnight,' said the boy. 'You will be safer that way.'

'How about me?' asked the Sawhorse.

'It won't hurt you to stand,' replied Tip; 'and, as you

can't sleep, you may as well watch out and see that no one comes near to disturb us.'

Then the boy stretched himself upon the grass beside the Pumpkinhead, and being greatly wearied by the journey was soon fast asleep.

6.

Jack Pumpkinhead's Ride

AT DAYBREAK, Tip was awakened by the Pumpkinhead. He rubbed the sleep from his eyes, bathed in a little brook, and ate a portion of his bread and cheese. Having thus prepared for a new day, the boy said:

'Let us start at once. Nine miles is quite a distance, but we ought to reach the Emerald City by noon if no accidents happen.'

So the Pumpkinhead was again perched on the back of

the Sawhorse and the journey was resumed.

The little party had travelled but a short two miles upon their way when the road of yellow brick was parted by a broad and swift river. Tip was puzzled how to cross over, but after a time he discovered a man in a ferryboat approaching from the other side of the stream.

When the man reached the bank, Tip asked:

'Will you row us to the other side?'

'Yes, if you have money,' returned the ferryman, whose face looked cross and disagreeable.

'But I have no money,' said Tip.

'None at all?' inquired the man.

'None at all,' answered the boy.

'Then I'll not break my back rowing you over,' said the ferryman decidedly.

'What a nice man!' remarked the Pumpkinhead smilingly.

The ferryman stared at him, but made no reply. Tip was trying to think, for it was a great disappointment to him to find his journey so suddenly brought to an end.

'I must certainly get to the Emerald City,' he said to the boatman, 'but how can I cross the river if you do not take me?'

The man laughed, and it was not a nice laugh.

'That wooden horse will float,' said he; 'and you can ride him across. As for the pumpkin-headed loon who accompanies you, let him sink or swim—it won't matter greatly which.'

'Don't worry about me,' said Jack, smiling pleasantly at

the crabbed ferryman? 'I'm sure I ought to float beautifully.'

Tip thought the experiment was worth making, and the Sawhorse, who did not know what danger meant, offered no objections whatever. So the boy led it down into the water and climbed upon its back. Jack also waded in up to his knees and grasped the tail of the horse, so that he might keep his pumpkin head above the water.

'Now,' said Tip, instructing the Sawhorse, 'if you wiggle your legs, you will probably swim; and if you swim, we shall probably reach the other side.'

The Sawhorse at once began to wiggle its legs, which acted as oars and moved the adventurers slowly across the river to the opposite side. So successful was the trip that presently they were climbing, wet and dripping, up the grassy bank.

Tip's trouser legs and shoes were thoroughly soaked, but the Sawhorse had floated so perfectly that from his knees up the boy was entirely dry. As for the Pumpkinhead, every stitch of his gorgeous clothing dripped water.

'The sun will soon dry us,' said Tip; 'and anyhow, we are now safely across, in spite of the ferryman, and can continue our journey.'

'I didn't mind swimming at all,' remarked the horse.

'Nor did I,' added Jack.

They soon regained the road of yellow brick, which proved to be a continuation of the road they had left on the other side, and then Tip once more mounted the Pumpkinhead on the back of the Sawhorse.

'If you ride fast,' said he, 'the wind will help to dry your clothing. I will hold on to the horse's tail and run after you. In this way we will all be dry in a very short time.'

'Then the horse must step lively,' said Jack.

'I'll do my best,' returned the Sawhorse, cheerfully.

Tip grasped the end of the branch that served as tail to the Sawhorse and called loudly, 'Get-up!'

The horse started at a good pace, and Tip followed behind. Then he decided they could go faster, so he shouted 'Trot!'

Now the Sawhorse remembered that this word was the command to go as fast as he could, so he began rocking along the road at a tremendous pace; and Tip, who was running faster than he ever had before in his life, had hard work to keep on his feet.

Soon he was out of breath and although he wanted to call 'Whoa!' to the horse, he found he could not get the word out of his throat. Then the end of the tail he was clutching, being nothing more than a dead branch, suddenly broke away, and the next minute the boy was rolling in the dust of the road, while the horse and its pumpkin-headed rider dashed on and quickly disappeared in the distance.

By the time Tip had picked himself up and cleared the dust from his throat so he could say 'Whoa!' there was no further need of saying it, for the horse was long since out of sight.

So he did the only sensible thing he could do. He sat down and took a good rest, and afterwards began walking along the road.

'Sometime I will surely overtake them,' he reflected,

'for the road will end at the gates of the Emerald City, and they can go no farther than that.'

Meantime Jack was holding fast to the post and the Sawhorse was tearing along the road like a racer. Neither of them knew Tip was left behind, for the Pumpkinhead did not look around and the Sawhorse couldn't.

As he rode, Jack noticed that the grass and trees had become a bright emerald-green in colour; so he guessed they were nearing the Emerald City even before the tall spires and domes came into sight.

At length a high wall of green stone, studded thick with emeralds, loomed up before them; and fearing the Sawhorse would not know enough to stop and so might smash them both against this wall, Jack ventured to cry 'Whoa!' as loud as he could.

So suddenly did the horse obey that, had it not been for his post, Jack would have been pitched off head foremost and his beautiful face ruined.

'That was a fast ride, dear Father!' he exclaimed; and then, hearing no reply, he turned around and discovered for the first time that Tip was not there.

This apparent desertion puzzled the Pumpkinhead and made him uneasy. And while he was wondering what had become of the boy, and what he ought to do next under such trying circumstances, the gateway in the green wall opened and a man came out.

This man was short and round, with a fat face that seemed remarkably good-natured. He was clothed all in green and wore a high, peaked green hat upon his head and green spectacles over his eyes. Bowing before the

Pumpkinhead, he said:

'I am the Guardian of the Gates of the Emerald City. May I inquire who you are and what is your business?'

'My name is Jack Pumpkinhead,' returned the other smilingly, 'but as to my business, I haven't the least idea in the world what it is.'

The Guardian of the Gates looked surprised and shook his head, as if dissatisfied with the reply.

'What are you, a man or a pumpkin?' he asked politely.

'Both, if you please,' answered Jack.

'And this wooden horse—is it alive?' questioned the Guardian.

The horse rolled one knotty eye upward and winked at Jack. Then it gave a prance and brought one leg down on the Guardian's toes.

'Ouch!' cried the man. 'I'm sorry I asked that question. But the answer is most convincing. Have you any errand, sir, in the Emerald City?'

'It seems to me that I have,' replied the Pumpkinhead seriously, 'but I cannot think what it is. My father knows all about it, but he is not here.'

'This is a strange affair—very strange!' declared the Guardian. 'But you seem harmless. Folks do not smile so delightfully when they mean mischief.'

'As for that,' said Jack, 'I cannot help my smile, for it is carved on my face with a jack-knife.'

'Well, come with me into my room,' resumed the Guardian 'and I will see what can be done for you.'

So Jack rode the Sawhorse through the gateway into a little room built into the wall. The Guardian pulled a bell cord, and presently a very tall soldier, clothed in a green uniform, entered from the opposite door. This Soldier carried a long green gun over his shoulder and had lovely green whiskers that fell quite to his knees. The Guardian at once addressed him:

'Here is a strange gentleman who doesn't know why he has come to the Emerald City or what he wants. Tell me, what shall we do with him?'

The Soldier with the Green Whiskers looked at Jack with much care and curiosity. Finally he shook his head so positively that little waves rippled down his whiskers, and then he said:

'I must take him to His Majesty the Scarecrow.'

'But what will His Majesty the Scarecrow do with him?' asked the Guardian of the Gates.

'That is His Majesty's business,' returned the Soldier. 'I have troubles enough of my own. All outside troubles must be turned over to His Majesty. So put the spectacles on this fellow, and I'll take him to the royal palace.'

So the Guardian opened a big box of spectacles and tried to fit a pair to Jack's great round eyes.

'I haven't a pair in stock that will really cover up those eyes,' said the little man with a sigh, 'and your head is so big that I shall be obliged to tie them on.'

'But why need I wear spectacles?' asked Jack.

'It's the fashion here,' said the Soldier, 'and they will keep you from being blinded by the glitter and glare of the gorgeous Emerald City.'

'Oh!' exclaimed Jack. 'Tie them on, by all means. I don't wish to be blinded.'

'Nor I!' broke in the Sawhorse; so a pair of green spectacles was quickly fastened over the bulging knots that served it for eyes.

Then the Soldier with the Green Whiskers led them through the inner gate, and they at once found themselves in the main street of the Emerald City.

Sparkling green gems ornamented the fronts of the beautiful houses, and the towers and turrets were all faced with emeralds. Even the green marble pavement glittered with precious stones.

However, the Pumpkinhead and the Sawhorse, knowing nothing of wealth and beauty, paid little attention to the wonderful sights they saw through their green spectacles. They calmly followed after the Green Soldier and scarcely noticed the crowds of green people who stared at them in surprise. When a green dog ran out and barked at them, the Sawhorse promptly kicked at it with its wooden leg and sent the little animal howling into one of the houses; but nothing more serious than this happened to interrupt their progress to the royal palace.

The Pumpkinhead wanted to ride up the green marble steps and straight into the Scarecrow's presence, but the Soldier would not permit that. So Jack dismounted, with much difficulty, and a servant led the Sawhorse around to the rear, while the Soldier with the Green Whiskers escorted the Pumpkinhead into the palace, by the front entrance.

The stranger was left in a handsomely furnished waiting room while the Soldier went to announce him. It so happened that at this hour His Majesty was at leisure and

greatly bored for want of something to do, so he ordered
his visitor to be shown in at once.

Jack felt no fear or embarrassment at meeting the ruler
of this magnificent city, for he was entirely ignorant of all
worldly customs. But when he entered the room and saw
for the first time His Majesty the Scarecrow seated upon
his glittering throne, he stopped short in amazement

7.

His Majesty the Scarecrow

I SUPPOSE EVERY READER OF THIS BOOK knows what a scarecrow is; but Jack Pumpkinhead, never having seen such a creation, was more surprised at meeting the remarkable King of the Emerald City than by any other one experience of his brief life.

His Majesty the Scarecrow was dressed in a suit of faded blue clothes, and his head was merely a small sack stuffed with straw, upon which eyes, ears, a nose, and a mouth had been rudely painted to represent a face. The clothes were also stuffed with straw, and that so unevenly or carelessly that His Majesty's legs and arms seemed more bumpy than necessary. On his hands were gloves with long fingers, and these were padded with cotton. Wisps of straw stuck out from the monarch's coat, and also from his neck and boot tops. Upon his head he wore a heavy golden crown set with sparkling jewels, and the weight of this crown caused his brow to sag in wrinkles, giving a thoughtful expression to the painted face. Indeed, the crown alone betokened majesty; in all else the Scarecrow King was but a simple scarecrow.

But if the strange appearance of His Majesty the Scarecrow seemed startling to Jack, no less wonderful was the sight of the Pumpkinhead to the Scarecrow. The purple trousers and pink waistcoat and red shirt hung loosely over the wooden joints Tip had manufactured, and the carved face on the pumpkin grinned perpetually, as if its wearer considered life the jolliest thing imaginable.

At first, indeed, His Majesty thought his queer visitor was laughing at him, and was inclined to resent such a liberty; but it was not without reason that the Scarecrow had attained the reputation of being the wisest personage in the Land of Oz. He made a more careful examination of his visitor, and soon discovered that Jack's features were carved into a smile and that he could not look grave if he wished to.

The King was the first to speak. After regarding Jack for some minutes he said, in a tone of wonder, 'Where on earth did you come from, and how do you happen to be alive?'

'I beg Your Majesty's pardon,' returned the Pumpkinhead, 'but I do not understand you.'

'What don't you understand?' asked the Scarecrow.

'Why, I don't understand your language. You see, I came from the Country of the Gillikins, so that I am a foreigner.'

'Ah, to be sure!' exclaimed the Scarecrow. 'I myself speak the language of the Munchkins, which is also the language of the Emerald City. But you, I suppose speak the language of the Pumpkinheads?'

'Exactly so, Your Majesty,' replied the other, bowing;

'so it will be impossible for us to understand one another.'

'That is unfortunate, certainly,' said the Scarecrow, thoughtfully. 'We must have an interpreter.'

'What is an interpreter?' asked Jack.

A person who understands both my language and your own. When I say anything, the interpreter can tell you what I mean; and when you say anything, the interpreter can tell me what *you* mean. For the interpreter can speak both languages as well as understand them.'

'That is certainly clever,' said Jack, greatly pleased at finding so simple a way out of the difficulty.

So the Scarecrow commanded the Soldier with the Green Whiskers to search among his people until he found one who understood the language of the Gillikins as well as the language of the Emerald City, and to bring that person to him at once.

When the Soldier had departed, the Scarecrow said: 'Won't you take a chair while we are waiting?'

'Your Majesty forgets that I cannot understand you,' replied the Pumpkinhead. 'If you wish me to sit down, you must make a sign for me to do so.'

The Scarecrow came down from his throne and rolled an armchair to a position behind the Pumpkinhead. Then he gave Jack a sudden push that sent him sprawling upon the cushions in so awkward a fashion that he doubled up like a jack-knife, and had hard work to untangle himself.

'Did you understand that sign?' asked His Majesty politely.

'Perfectly,' declared Jack, reaching up his arms to turn his head to the front, the pumpkin having twisted around upon the stick that supported it.

'You seem hastily made,' remarked the Scarecrow, watching Jack's efforts to straighten himself.

'Not more so than Your Majesty,' was the frank reply.

'There is this difference between us,' said the Scarecrow, 'that whereas I will bend but not break, you will break but not bend.'

At this moment the Soldier returned, leading a young girl by the hand. She seemed very sweet and modest, having a pretty face and beautiful green eyes and hair. A dainty green-silk skirt reached to her knees, showing silk stockings embroidered with pea pods, and green satin slippers with bunches of lettuce for decorations instead of bows or buckles. Upon her silken waist, clover leaves were embroidered, and she wore a jaunty little jacket trimmed with sparkling emeralds of a uniform size.

'Why, it's little Jellia Jamb!' exclaimed the Scarecrow, as the green maiden bowed her pretty head before him. 'Do you understand the language of the Gillikins, my dear?'

'Yes, Your Majesty,' she answered, 'for I was born in the North Country.'

'Then you shall be our interpreter,' said the Scarecrow, 'and explain to this Pumpkinhead all that I say, and also explain to me all that *he* says. Is this arrangement satisfactory?' he asked, turning towards his guest.

'Very satisfactory indeed,' was the reply.

'Then ask him, to begin with,' resumed the Scarecrow, turning to Jellia, 'what brought him to the Emerald City.'

But instead of this the girl, who had been staring at Jack,

said to him:

'You are certainly a wonderful creature. Who made you?'

'A boy named Tip,' answered Jack.

'What does he say?' inquired the Scarecrow. 'My ears must have deceived me. What did he say?'

'He says that Your Majesty's brains seem to have come loose,' replied the girl, demurely.

The Scarecrow moved uneasily upon his throne, and felt of his head with his left hand.

'What a fine thing it is to understand two different languages,' he said, with a perplexed sigh. 'Ask him, my dear, if he has any objection to being put in jail for insulting the ruler of the Emerald City.'

'I didn't insult you!' protested Jack, indignantly.

'Tut-tut!' cautioned the Scarecrow. 'Wait until Jellia translates my speech. What have we got an interpreter for, if you break out in this rash way?'

'All right, I'll wait,' replied the Pumpkinhead, in a surly tone, although his face smiled as genially as ever. 'Translate the speech, young woman.'

'His Majesty asks if you are hungry,' said Jellia.

'Oh, not at all!' answered Jack more pleasantly, 'for it is impossible for me to eat.'

'It's the same way with me,' remarked the Scarecrow. 'What did he say, Jellia, my dear?'

'He asked if you were aware that one of your eyes is painted larger than the other,' said the girl, mischievously.

'Don't you believe her, Your Majesty,' cried Jack.

'Oh, I don't,' answered the Scarecrow calmly. Then,

casting a sharp look at the girl, he asked:

'Are you quite certain you understand the languages of both the Gillikins and the Munchkins?'

'Quite certain, Your Majesty,' said Jellia Jamb, trying hard not to laugh in the face of royalty.

'Then how is it that I seem to understand them myself?' inquired the Scarecrow.

'Because they are one and the same!' declared the girl, now laughing merrily. 'Does not Your Majesty know that in the Land of Oz but one language is spoken?'

'Is it inded so?' cried the Scarecrow, much relieved to hear this. 'Then I might easily have been my own interpreter!'

'It was all my fault, Your Majesty,' said Jack, looking rather foolish, 'I thought we must surely speak different languages, since we came from different countries.'

'This should be a warning to you never to think,' returned the Scarecrow severely. 'For unless one can think wisely, it is better to remain a dummy—which you most certainly are.'

'I am! I surely am!' agreed the Pumpkinhead.

'It seems to me,' continued the Scarecrow, more mildly, 'that your manufacturer spoiled some good pies to create an indifferent man.'

'I assure Your Majesty, I did not ask to be created,' answered Jack.

'Ah! It was the same in my case,' said the King pleasantly. 'And so, as we differ from all ordinary people, let us become friends.'

'With all my heart!' exclaimed Jack.

'What! Have you a heart?' asked the Scarecrow, surprised.

'No; that was only imagination—I might say, a figure of speech,' said the other.

'Your most prominent figure seems to be a figure of wood,' remarked the Scarecrow, looking Jack up and down.

'To be sure!' said Jack, without in the least comprehending.

His Majesty then dismissed Jellia Jamb and the Soldier with the Green Whiskers, and when they were gone he took his new friend by the arm and led him into the courtyard to play a game of quoits.

8.

General Jinjur's Army of Revolt

TIP WAS SO ANXIOUS TO REJOIN his man Jack and the Sawhorse that he walked a full half the distance to the Emerald City without stopping to rest. Then he discovered that he was hungry, and that he had eaten all the crackers and cheese he had provided for his trip.

While he was wondering what to do about this, he came upon a girl sitting by the roadside. She wore a costume that struck the boy as being remarkably brilliant; her silken waist was of emerald green and her skirt of four distinct colours—blue in front, yellow at the left side, red at the back, and purple at the right side. Fastening the waist in front were four buttons; the top one was blue, the next yellow, a third red, and the last purple.

The splendour of this dress was such that Tip stared for some moments before his eyes were attracted by the pretty face above it. Yes, the face was pretty enough, he decided; but it wore an expression of discontent coupled with defiance.

While the boy stared, the girl looked at him calmly. A lunch basket stood beside her, and she held a dainty sandwich in one hand and a hard-boiled egg in the other, eating with an evident appetite that aroused Tip's sympathy.

He was just about to ask for a share of the luncheon when the girl stood up and brushed away the crumbs.

'There!' said she. 'It's time for me to go. Carry that basket for me, and help yourself to its contents if you are hungry.'

Tip seized the basket eagerly and began to eat. He followed the strange girl for a time without bothering to ask questions. She walked along before him with swift strides, and there was about her an air of decision and importance.

'Thank you very much for the sandwiches,' said Tip, as he trotted along. 'May I ask your name?'

'I am General Jinjur,' was the brief reply.

'Oh!' exclaimed the boy. 'What sort of general?'

'I command the Army of Revolt in this war,' answered the General, with unnecessary sharpness.

'Oh!' he again exclaimed. 'I didn't know there was a war.'

'You were not supposed to know it,' she returned, 'for we have kept it a secret. And considering that our army is composed entirely of girls,' she added with some pride, 'it is surely a remarkable thing that our revolt is not yet discovered.'

'It is indeed,' said Tip. 'But where is your army?'

'About a mile from here,' said General Jinjur. 'The forces have assembled from all parts of the Land of Oz, at my express command. For this is the day we are to conquer His Majesty the Scarecrow, and wrest from him the throne.

The Army of Revolt only awaits my coming to march upon the Emerald City.'

'Well!' declared Tip, drawing a long breath, 'this is certainly surprising! May I ask why you wish to conquer His Majesty the Scarecrow?'

'Because the Emerald City has been ruled by men long enough, for one reason,' said the girl. 'Moreover, the city glitters with beautiful gems, which might far better be used for rings, bracelets, and necklaces; and there is enough money in the King's treasury to buy every girl in our army a dozen new gowns. So we intend to conquer the city and run the government to suit ourselves.'

Jinjur spoke these words with an eagerness and decision that proved she was in earnest.

'But war is a terrible thing,' said Tip, thoughtfully.

'This war will be pleasant,' replied the girl.

'Many of you will be slain!'

'Oh no,' said Jinjur. 'What man would oppose a girl or dare to harm her? And there is not an ugly face in my entire Army.'

Tip laughed.

'Perhaps you are right,' said he. 'But the Guardian of the Gate is considered a faithful guardian, and the King's Army will not let the city be conquered without a struggle.'

'The Army is old and feeble,' replied General Jinjur, scornfully. 'His strength has all been used to grow whiskers, and his wife has such a temper that she has already pulled more than half of them out by the roots. When the Wonderful Wizard reigned, the Soldier with the Green

Whiskers was a very good Royal Army, for people feared the Wizard. But no one is afraid of the Scarecrow, so his Royal Army doesn't count for much in time of war.'

After this conversation they proceeded for some distance in silence. Before long they reached a large clearing in the forest where fully four hundred girls were assembled. They were all laughing and talking together as gaily as if they had gathered for a picnic.

They were divided into four companies, and Tip noticed that all were dressed in costumes similar to that worn by General Jinjur. The only real difference was that while those girls from the Munchkin Country had the blue strip in front of their skirts, those from the Country of the Quadlings had the red strip in front, and those from the Country of the Winkies had the yellow strip in front. The Gillikin girls wore the purple strip in front. All had green waists, representing the Emerald City they intended to conquer, and the top button on each waist indicated by its colour which country the wearer came from.

Tip thought this strange army bore no weapons whatever, but in this he was wrong. For each girl had stuck through the knot of her back hair two long, glittering knitting needles.

General Jinjur immediately mounted the stump of a tree and addressed her army.

'Friends, fellow citizens, and girls!' she said. 'We are about to begin our great revolt against the men of Oz! We march to conquer the Emerald City—to dethrone the Scarecrow King—to acquire thousands of gorgeous gems— to rifle the royal treasury—and to obtain power over our former oppressors!'

'Hurrah!' said those who had listened; but Tip thought most of the army was too much engaged in chattering to pay attention to the General's words.

The command to march was now given, and the girls formed themselves into four bands, or companies, and set off with eager strides towards the Emerald City.

The boy followed after them, carrying several baskets and wraps and packages which various members of the Army of Revolt had placed in his care. It was not long before they came to the green granite walls of the city and halted before the gateway.

The Guardian of the Gate at once came out and looked at them curiously, as if a circus had come to town. He carried a bunch of keys swung round his neck by a golden chain; his hands were thrust carelessly into his pockets, and he seemed to have no idea at all that the city was threatened by rebels. Speaking pleasantly to the girls, he said:

'Good morning, my dears! What can I do for you?'

'Surrender instantly!' answered General Jinjur, standing before him and frowning as terribly as her pretty face would allow her to.

'Surrender!' echoed the man, astounded. 'Why, it's impossible. It's against the law! I never heard of such a thing in my life.'

'Still, you must surrender!' exclaimed the General, fiercely. 'We are revolting!'

'You don't look it,' said the Guardian, gazing from one to another admiringly.

'But we are!' cried Jinjur, stamping her foot impatiently. 'We mean to conquer the Emerald City!'

'Good gracious!' returned the surprised Guardian of the Gates. 'What a nonsensical idea! Go home to your mothers, my good girls, and milk the cows and bake the bread. Don't you know it's a dangerous thing to conquer a city?'

'We are not afraid!' responded the General; and she looked so determined, the Guardian felt uneasy.

So he rang the bell for the Soldier with the Green Whiskers, and the next minute was sorry he had done so. For immediately he was surrounded by a crowd of girls who drew the knitting needles from their hair and began jabbing them at the Guardian.

The poor man howled loudly for mercy and made no resistance when Jinjur drew the bunch of keys from around his neck.

Followed by her Army, the General now rushed to the gateway, where she was confronted by the Royal Army of Oz—which was the other name for the Soldier with the Green Whiskers.

'Halt!' he cried, and pointed his long gun full in the face of the leader.

Some of the girls screamed and ran back, but General Jinjur bravely stood her ground and said reproachfully:

'Why, how now? Would you shoot a poor defenceless girl?'

'No,' replied the Soldier, 'for my gun isn't loaded.'

'Not loaded?'

'No—for fear of accidents. And I've forgotten where

I hid the powder and shot to load it with. But if you'll wait a short time I'll try to hunt them up.'

'Don't trouble yourself,' said Jinjur cheerfully. Then she turned to her army and cried:

'Girls, the gun isn't loaded!'

'Hooray,' shrieked the rebels, delighted at this good news, and they proceeded to rush on the Soldier with the Green Whiskers in such a mob that it was a wonder they didn't stick the knitting needles into one another.

But the Royal Army of Oz was too much afraid of girls to meet the onslaught. He simply turned about and ran with all his might through the gate and towards the royal palace, while General Jinjur and her mob flocked into the unprotected city.

In this way the Emerald City was captured without a drop of blood being spilled. The Army of Revolt had become an Army of Conquerors!

9.
The Scarecrow Plans
an Escape

Tɪᴘ ꜱʟɪᴘᴘᴇᴅ ᴀᴡᴀʏ ꜰʀᴏᴍ ᴛʜᴇ ɢɪʀʟꜱ and followed swiftly after the Soldier with the Green Whiskers. The invading army entered the city more slowly, for they stopped to dig emeralds out of the walls and paving stones with the points of their knitting needles. So the Soldier and the boy reached the palace before the news had spread that the city was conquered.

The Scarecrow and Jack Pumpkinhead were still playing at quoits in the courtyard when the game was interrupted by the abrupt entrance of the Royal Army of Oz, who came flying in without hat or gun.

'Tally one for me,' said the Scarecrow calmly. 'What's wrong, my man?' he asked the Soldier.

'Oh! Your Majesty, Your Majesty! The city is conquered!' gasped the Royal Army, who was all out of breath.

'This is quite sudden,' said the Scarecrow. 'But please go and bar all the doors and windows of the palace, while I show Jack here how to throw a quoit.'

The Soldier hastened to do this, while Tip, who had

arrived at his heels, remained in the courtyard to look at the Scarecrow with wondering eyes.

His Majesty continued to throw the quoits as coolly as if no danger threatened his throne, but the Pumpkinhead, having caught sight of Tip, ambled towards the boy as fast as his wooden legs would go.

'Good afternoon, noble parent!' he cried, delightedly. 'I'm glad to see you are here. That terrible Sawhorse ran away with me.'

'I suspected it,' said Tip. 'Did you get hurt? Are you cracked at all?'

'No, I arrived safely,' answered Jack, 'and His Majesty has been very kind indeed to me.'

At this moment the Soldier with the Green Wiskers returned, and the Scarecrow asked, 'By the way, who has conquered me?'

'A regiment of girls, gathered from the four corners of the Land of Oz,' replied the Soldier, still pale with fear.

'But where was my standing Army at the time?' inquired his Majesty, looking at the Soldier gravely.

'Your standing Army was running,' answered the fellow honestly, 'for no man could face the terrible weapons of the invaders.'

'Well,' said the Scarecrow, after a moment's thought, 'I don't mind much the loss of my throne, for it's a tiresome job to rule over the Emerald City. And this crown is so heavy that it makes my head ache. But I hope the conquerors have no intention of injuring me, just because I happen to be the King.'

'I heard them say,' remarked Tip, with some hesitation,

'that they intend to make a rag carpet of your outside and stuff their sofa cusions with your inside.'

'Then I am really in danger,' declared his Majesty positively, 'and it will be wise for me to consider a means to escape.'

'Where can you go?' asked Jack Pumpkinhead.

'Why, to my friend the Tin Woodman, who rules over the Winkies and calls himself their Emperor,' was the answer. 'I am sure he will protect me.'

Tip was looking out of the window.

'The palace is surrounded by the enemy,' said he. 'It is too late to escape. They would soon tear you to pieces.'

The Scarecrow sighed.

'In an emergency,' he announced, 'it is always a good thing to pause and reflect. Please excuse me while I pause and reflect.'

'But we also are in danger,' said the Pumpkinhead anxiously. 'If any of these girls understand cooking my end is not far off!'

'Nonsense!' exclaimed the Scarecrow. 'They're too busy to cook, even if they know how!'

'But should I remain here a prisoner for any length of time,' protested Jack, 'I'm liable to spoil.'

'Ah! then you would not be fit to associate with,' returned the Scarecrow. 'The matter is more serious than I suspected.'

'You,' said the Pumpkinhead, gloomily, 'are liable to live for many years. My life is necessarily short. So I must take advantage of the few days I have.'

'There, there! Don't worry,' answered the Scarecrow

soothingly. 'If you'll keep quiet long enough for me to think, I'll try to find a way for us to escape.'

So the others waited in patient silence while the Scarecrow walked to a corner and stood with his face to the wall for a good five minutes. At the end of that time he faced them with a more cheerful expression upon his painted face.

'Where is the Sawhorse you rode here?' he asked the Pumpkinhead.

'Why, I said he was a jewel, and so your man locked him up in the royal treasury,' said Jack.

'It was the only place I could think of, Your Majesty,' added the Soldier, fearing he'd made a blunder.

'It pleases me very much,' said the Scarecrow. 'Has the animal been fed?'

'Oh yes; I gave him a heaping peck of sawdust.'

'Excellent!' cried the Scarecrow. 'Bring the horse here at once.'

The Soldier hastened away, and presently they heard the clattering of the horse's wooden legs upon the pavement as he was led into the courtyard.

His Majesty regarded the steed critically.

'He doesn't seem especially graceful,' he remarked musingly, 'but I suppose he can run?'

'He can indeed,' said Tip, gazing upon the Sawhorse admiringly.

'Then, bearing us upon his back, he must make a dash through the ranks of the rebels and carry us to my friend the Tin Woodman,' said the Scarecrow.

'He can't carry four!' objected Tip.

'No, but he may be induced to carry three,' said His Majesty. 'I shall therefore leave my Royal Army behind. For, from the ease with which he was conquered, I have little confidence in his powers.'

'Still, he can run,' declared Tip, laughing.

'I expected this blow,' said the Soldier sulkily, 'but I can bear it. I shall disguise myself by cutting off my lovely green whiskers. And, after all, it is no more dangerous to face those reckless girls than to ride this fiery, untamed wooden horse!'

'Perhaps you are right,' observed His Majesty. 'But for my part, not being a soldier, I am fond of danger. Now, my boy, you must mount first. And please sit as close to the horse's neck as possible.'

Tip climbed quickly to his place, and the Soldier and the Scarecrow managed to hoist the Pumpkinhead to a seat just behind him. There remained so little space for the King that he was liable to fall off as soon as the horse started.

'Fetch a clothesline,' said the King to his Army, 'and tie us all together. Then if one falls off, we will all fall off.'

And while the Soldier was gone for the clothesline, His Majesty continued, 'It is well for me to be careful, for my very existence is in danger.'

'I have to be as careful as you do,' said Jack.

'Not exactly,' replied the Scarecrow; 'for if anything happened to me, that would be the end of me. But if anything happened to you, they could use you for seed.'

The Soldier now returned with a long line and tied all three firmly together, also lashing them to the body of the

Sawhorse; so there seemed little danger of their tumbling off.

'Now throw open the gates,' commanded the Scarecrow, 'and we will make a dash to liberty or death.'

The courtyard in which they were standing was located in the centre of the great palace, which surrounded it on all sides. But in one place a passage led to an outer gateway, which the Soldier had barred by order of his sovereign. It was through this gateway His Majesty proposed to escape, and the Royal Army now led the Sawhorse along the passage and unbarred the gate, which swung backward with a crash.

'Now,' said Tip to the horse, 'you must save us all. Run as fast as you can for the gate of the city, and don't let anything stop you.'

'All right!' answered the Sawhorse gruffly, and dashed away so suddenly that Tip had to gasp for breath and hold firmly to the post he had driven into the creature's neck.

Several of the girls who stood outside guarding the palace, were knocked over by the Sawhorse's mad rush. Others ran screaming out of the way, and only one or two jabbed their knitting needles frantically at the escaping prisoners. Tip got one small prick in his left arm, which smarted for an hour afterwards; but the needles had no effect upon the Scarecrow or Jack Pumpkinhead.

As for the Sawhorse, he made a wonderful record, upsetting a fruit cart, overturning several meek-looking men, and finally bowling over the new Guardian of the Gate— a fussy little fat woman appointed by General Jinjur.

Nor did the impetuous charger stop then. Once outside

the walls of the Emerald City, he dashed along the road to the West with fast and violent leaps that shook the breath out of the boy and filled the Scarecrow with wonder.

Jack had ridden at this mad rate once before, so he devoted every effort to holding, with both hands, his pumpkin head upon its stick, enduring meantime the dreadful jolting with the courage of a philosopher.

'Slow him up! Slow him up!' shouted the Scarecrow. 'My straw is all shaking down into my legs.'

But Tip had no breath to speak, so the Sawhorse continued his wild career unchecked and with unabated speed.

Presently they came to the banks of a wide river, and without a pause the wooden steed gave one final leap and launched them all in mid-air.

A second later they were rolling, splashing, and bobbing about in the water, the horse struggling frantically to find a rest for its feet, and its riders being first plunged beneath the rapid current and then floating on the surface like corks.

10.

The Journey to the Tin Woodman

TIP WAS WELL SOAKED and dripping water from every angle of his body, but he managed to lean forward and shout in the ear of the Sawhorse:

'Keep still, you fool! Keep still!'

The horse at once ceased struggling and floated calmly

upon the surface, its wooden body being as buoyant as a raft.

'What does that word "fool" mean?' inquired the horse.

'It is a term of reproach,' answered Tip, somewhat ashamed of the expression. 'I use it when I am angry.'

'Then it pleases me to be able to call you a fool, in return,' said the horse. 'For I did not make the river, nor put it in our way; so only a term of reproach is fit for one who becomes angry with me for falling into the water.'

'That is true,' replied Tip, 'so I will acknowledge myself in the wrong.' Then he called out to the Pumpkinhead, 'Are you all right, Jack?'

There was no reply. So the boy called to the King, 'Are you all right, Your Majesty?'

The Scarecrow groaned.

'I'm all wrong, somehow,' he said, in a weak voice, 'How very wet this water is!'

Tip was bound so tightly by the cord that he could not turn his head to look at his companions; so he said to the Sawhorse, 'Paddle with your legs towards the shore.'

The horse obeyed, and although their progress was slow, they finally reached the opposite river bank at a place where it was low enough to enable the creature to scramble upon dry land.

With some difficulty the boy managed to get his knife out of his pocket and cut the cords that bound the riders to one another and to the wooden horse. He heard the Scarecraw fall to the ground with a mushy sound, and then he himself quickly dismounted and looked at his friend Jack.

The wooden body, with its gorgeous clothing, still sat upright upon the horse's back; but the pumpkin head was gone, and only the sharpened stick that served for a neck was visible. As for the Scarecrow, the straw in his body had shaken down with the jolting and packed itself into his legs and the lower part of his body, which appeared very plump and round, while his upper half seemed like an empty sack. Upon his head the Scarecrow still wore the heavy crown, which had been sewed on to prevent his losing it; but the head was now so damp and limp that the weight of the gold and jewels sagged forward and crushed the painted face into a mass of wrinkles.

Tip would have laughed, had he not been so anxious about his man Jack. But the Scarecrow, however damaged, was all there, while the pumpkin head that was so necessary to Jack's existence was missing; so the boy seized a long pole that fortunately lay near at hand and anxiously turned again towards the river.

Far out upon the waters he sighted the golden hue of the pumpkin, which gently bobbed up and down with the motion of the waves. At that moment it was quite out of Tip's reach, but after a time it floated nearer and still nearer, until the boy was able to reach it with his pole and draw it to the shore. Then he brought it to the top of the bank, carefully wiped the water from its pumpkin face with his handkerchief, and ran with it to Jack and replaced the head on the man's neck.

'Dear me!' were Jack's first words. 'What a dreadful experience! I wonder if water is liable to spoil pumpkins?'

Tip did not think a reply was necessary, for he knew

that the Scarecrow also stood in need of his help. So he carefully removed the straw from the King's body and legs, and spread it out in the sun to dry. The wet clothing he hung over the body of the Sawhorse.

'If water spoils pumpkins,' observed Jack, with a deep sigh, 'then my days are numbered.'

'I've never noticed that water spoils pumpkins,' returned Tip, 'unless the water happens to be boiling. If your head isn't cracked, my friend, you must be in fairly good condition.'

'Oh, my head isn't cracked in the least,' declared Jack, more cheerfully.

'Then don't worry,' retorted the boy. 'Care once killed a cat.'

'Then,' said Jack seriously, 'I am very glad indeed that I am not a cat.'

The sun was fast drying their clothing, and Tip stirred up His Majesty's straw so that the warm rays might absorb the moisture and make it as crisp and dry as ever. When this had been accomplished, he stuffed the Scarecrow into symmetrical shape and smoothed out his face, so that he wore his usual gay and charming expression.

'Thank you very much,' said the monarch brightly, as he walked about and found himself to be well balanced. 'There are several distinct advantages in being a scarecrow. For if one has friends near at hand to repair damages, nothing very serious can happen to you.'

'I wonder if hot sunshine is liable to crack pumpkins,' said Jack, with an anxious ring in his voice.

'Not at all, not at all!' replied the Scarecrow gaily. 'All

you need fear, my boy, is old age. When your golden youth has decayed, we shall quickly part company—but you needn't look forward to it; we'll discover the fact ourselves and notify you. But come! let us resume our journey. I am anxious to greet my friend the Tin Woodman.'

So they remounted the Sawhorse, Tip holding to the post, the Pumpkinhead clinging to Tip and the Scarecrow with both arms around the wooden form of Jack.

'Go slowly, for now there is no danger of pursuit,' said Tip to his steed.

'All right!' responded the creature, in a rather gruff voice.

'Aren't you a little hoarse?' asked Jack politely.

The Sawhorse gave an angry prance and rolled one knotty eye backward towards Tip.

'See here,' he growled, 'can't you protect me from insult?'

'To be sure!' answered Tip, soothingly. 'I am sure Jack meant no harm. And it will not do for us to quarrel, you know; we must all remain good friends.'

'I'll have nothing more to do with that Pumpkinhead,' declared the Sawhorse viciously; 'he loses his head too easily to suit me.'

There seemed no fitting reply to this speech, so for a time they rode along in silence.

After a while the Scarecrow remarked:

'This reminds me of old times. It was upon this grassy knoll that I once saved Dorothy from the Stinging Bees of the Wicked Witch of the West.'

'Do Stinging Bees injure pumpkins?' asked Jack, glancing around fearfully.

'They are all dead, so it doesn't matter,' replied the Scarecrow. 'And here is where Nick Chopper destroyed the Wicked Witch's Grey Wolves.'

'Who was Nick Chopper?' asked Tip.

'That is the name of my friend the Tin Woodman,' answered His Majesty. 'And here is where the Winged Monkeys captured and bound us, and flew away with little Dorothy,' he continued, after they had travelled a little way farther.

'Do Winged Monkeys ever eat pumpkins?' asked Jack, with a shiver of fear.

'I do not know; but you have little cause to worry, for the Winged Monkeys are now the slaves of Glinda the Good, who owns the Golden Cap that commands their services,' said the Scarecrow reflectively.

Then the stuffed monarch became lost in thought, recalling the days of past adventures. And the Sawhorse rocked and rolled over the flower-strewn fields and carried its riders swiftly upon their way.

Twilight fell bye and bye, and then the dark shadows of night. So Tip stopped the horse and they all proceeded to dismount.

'I'm tired out,' said the boy yawning wearily, 'and the grass is soft and cool. Let's lie down here and sleep until morning.'

'I can't sleep,' said Jack.

'I never do,' said the Scarecrow.

'I do not know what sleep is,' said the Sawhorse.

'Still, we must have consideration for this poor boy, who is made of flesh and blood and bone, and gets tired,' suggested the Scarecrow, in his usual thoughtful manner. 'I remember it was the same way with little Dorothy. We always had to sit through the night while she slept.'

'I'm sorry,' said Tip meekly, 'but I can't help it. And I'm dreadfully hungry, too!'

'Here is a new danger!' remarked Jack gloomily. 'I hope you are not fond of eating pumpkins.'

'Not unless they're stewed and made into pies,' answered Tip, laughing. 'So have no fears, friend Jack.'

'What a coward that Pumpkinhead is!' said the Sawhorse scornfully.

'You might be a coward yourself, if you knew you were liable to spoil!' retorted Jack angrily.

'There, there!' interrupted the Scarecrow; 'don't let us quarrel. We all have our weaknesses, dear friends, so we must strive to be considerate of one another. And since this poor boy is hungry and has nothing whatever to eat, let us all remain quiet and allow him to sleep; for it is said that in sleep a mortal may forget even hunger.'

'Thank you!' exclaimed Tip gratefully. 'Your Majesty is fully as good as you are wise, and that is saying a good deal!'

He then stretched himself upon the grass and, using the stuffed form of the Scarecrow for a pillow, was presently fast asleep.

11.

A Nickel-Plated Emperor

TIP AWOKE SOON AFTER DAWN, but the Scarecrow had already risen and plucked, with his clumsy fingers, a double handful of ripe berries from some bushes nearby. These the boy ate greedily, finding them an ample breakfast; then the little party set out again.

After an hour's ride they reached the summit of a hill from whence they espied the City of the Winkies; they noted the tall domes of the Emperor's palace rising from the clusters of more modest dwellings.

The Scarecrow became greatly animated at this sight, and exclaimed, 'How delighted I shall be to see my old friend the Tin Woodman again!'

'Is your friend the Tin Woodman the Emperor of the Winkies?' asked the Sawhorse.

'Yes, indeed. They invited him to rule over them soon after the Wicked Witch was destroyed; and as Nick Chopper has the best heart in all the world, I am sure he has proved an excellent and able emperor.'

'I thought that "Emperor" was the title of a person who rules an empire,' said Tip, 'and the Country of the

Winkies is only a kingdom.'

'Don't mention that to the Tin Woodman!' exclaimed the Scarecrow earnestly. 'You would hurt his feelings terribly. He is a proud man, as he has every reason to be, and it pleases him to be termed Emperor rather than King.'

'I'm sure it makes no difference to me,' said the boy.

The Sawhorse now ambled forward at a pace so fast that its riders had hard work to stick on its back, so there was little further conversation until they drew up beside the palace steps.

An aged Winkie, dressed in a uniform of silver cloth, came forward to assist them to alight. Said the Scarecrow to this person, 'Show us at once to your master the Emperor.'

The man looked from one to another of the party in an embarrassed way, and finally answered:

'I fear I must ask you to wait for a time. The Emperor is not receiving this morning.'

'How is that?' inquired the Scarecrow anxiously. 'I hope nothing has happened to him.'

'Oh no—nothing serious,' returned the man. 'But this is His Majesty's day for being polished, and just now his august presence is thickly smeared with polishing cream.'

'Oh, I see!' cried the Scarecrow, greatly reassured. 'My friend was always inclined to be a dandy, and I suppose he is prouder than ever of his appearance.'

'He is indeed,' said the man, with a polite bow. 'Our mighty Emperor has lately caused himself to be nickel-plated.'

'Good gracious!' the Scarecrow exclaimed at hearing

this. 'If his wit bears the same polish, how sparkling it must be! But show us in—I'm sure the Emperor will receive us, even in his present state.'

'The Emperor's state is always magnificent,' said the man. 'But I will venture to tell him of your arrival, and will receive his commands concerning you.'

So the party followed the servant into a splendid ante-room, and the Sawhorse ambled awkwardly after them, having no knowledge that a horse might be expected to remain outside.

The travellers were at first somewhat awed by their surroundings, and even the Scarecrow seemed impressed as he examined the rich hangings of silver cloth caught up into knots and fastened with tiny silver axes. Upon a handsome centre table stood a large silver oil-can, richly engraved with scenes from the past adventures of the Tin Woodman, Dorothy, the Cowardly Lion, and the Scarecrow, the lines of the engraving being traced upon the silver in yellow gold. On the walls hung several portraits, that of the Scarecrow seeming to be the most prominent and carefully executed, while a large painting of the famous Wizard of Oz, in the act of presenting the Tin Woodman with a heart, covered almost one entire end of the room.

While the visitors gazed at these things in silent admiration, they suddenly heard a loud voice exclaiming:

'Well! well! well! What a great surprise!'

And then the door burst open, and Nick Chopper rushed into their midst and caught the Scarecrow in a close and loving embrace.

'My dear old friend! My noble comrade!' cried the Tin Woodman joyfully. 'How delighted I am to meet you once again!'

And then he released the Scarecrow and held him at arm's length while he surveyed the beloved, painted features.

But alas! the face of the Scarecrow and many portions of his body bore great blotches of polishing cream; for the Tin Woodman, in his eagerness to welcome his friend, had quite forgotten the condition of his person and had rubbed off the polish from his own body to that of his comrade.

'Dear me!' said the Scarecrow dolefully. 'What a mess I'm in!'

'Never mind, my friend,' returned the Tin Woodman, I'll send you to my imperial laundry, and you'll come out as good as new.'

'Won't I be mangled?' asked the Scarecrow.

'No, indeed!' was the reply. 'But tell me, how came Your Majesty here? And who are your companions?'

The Scarecrow, with great politeness, introduced Tip and Jack Pumpkinhead, and the latter seemed to interest the Tin Woodman greatly.

'You are not very substantial, I must admit,' said the Emperor, 'but you are certainly unusual, and worthy to become a member of our select society.'

'I thank your Majesty,' said Jack humbly.

'I hope you are enjoying good health?' continued the Woodman.

'At present, yes,' replied the Pumpkinhead, with a sigh, 'but I am in constant terror of the day when I shall spoil.'

'Nonsense!' said the Emperor, but in a kindly, sympathetic tone. 'Do not, I beg of you, dampen today's sun with the showers of tomorrow. For before your head has time to spoil you can have it canned, and in that way it may be preserved indefinitely.'

Tip, during this conversation, was looking at the Woodman with undisguised amazement, and noticed that the celebrated Emperor of the Winkies was composed entirely of tin, neatly soldered and riveted together into the form of a man. He rattled and clanked a little as he moved, but in the main he seemed to be most cleverly constructed, and his appearance was only marred by the coating of polishing paste that covered him from head to foot.

The boy's intent gaze caused the Tin Woodman to remember that he was not in the most presentable condition, so he begged his friends to excuse him while he retired to his private apartment and allowed his servants to polish him. This was accomplished in a short time; and when the Emperor returned, his nickel-plated body shone so magnificently that the Scarecrow heartily congratulated him on his appearance.

'That nickel-plate was, I confess, a happy thought,' said Nick, 'and it was the more necessary because I had become somewhat scratched during my adventurous experiences. You will observe this engraved star upon my left breast. It not only indicates where my excellent heart lies, but covers very neatly the patch made by the wonderful Wizard when he placed that valued organ in my breast with his own skilful hands.'

'Is your heart then a hand organ?' asked the Pumpkin-head curiously.

'By no means,' responded the Emperor with dignity. 'It is, I am convinced, a truly genuine heart, although somewhat larger and warmer than most people possess.'

Then he turned to the Scarecrow and asked:

'Are your subjects happy and contented, my dear friend?'

'I cannot say,' was the reply, 'for the girls of Oz have driven me out of the Emerald City.'

'Great goodness!' cried the Tin Woodman. 'What a calamity! They surely do not complain of your wise and gracious rule?'

'No; but they say it is a poor rule that doesn't work both ways,' answered the Scarecrow; 'and these females are also of the opinion that men have ruled the land long enough. So they have captured my city, robbed the treasury of all its jewels, and are running things to suit themselves.'

'Dear me! What an extraordinary idea!' cried the Emperor, who was both shocked and surprised.

'And I heard some of them say,' said Tip, 'that they intend to march here and capture the castle and city of the Tin Woodman.'

'Ah! we must not give them time to do that,' said the Emperor quickly. 'We will go at once and recapture the Emerald City and place the Scarecrow again upon his throne.'

'I was sure you would help me,' remarked the Scarecrow in a pleased voice. 'How large an army can you assemble?'

'We do not need an army,' replied the Woodman. 'We four, with the aid of my gleaming axe, are enough to strike terror into the hearts of the rebels.'

'We five,' corrected the Pumpkinhead.

'Five?' repeated the Tin Woodman.

'Yes; the Sawhorse is brave and fearless,' answered Jack, forgetting his recent quarrel with the horse.

The Tin Woodman looked around him in a puzzled way, for the Sawhorse had until now remained quietly standing in a corner, where the Emperor had not noticed him. Tip immediately called the odd-looking creature to them, and it approached so awkwardly that it nearly upset the beautiful centre table and the engraved oil-can.

'I begin to think,' remarked the Tin Woodman as he looked earnestly at the Sawhorse, 'that wonders will never cease! How came this creature alive?'

'I did it with a magic powder,' modestly asserted the boy, 'and the Sawhorse has been very useful to us.'

'He enabled us to escape the rebels,' added the Scarecrow.

'Then we must surely accept him as a comrade,' declared the Emperor. 'A live Sawhorse is a distinct novelty, and should prove an interesting study. Does he know anything?'

'Well, I cannot claim any great experience in life,' the Sawhorse answered for himself, 'but I seem to learn very quickly; and it often occurs to me that I know more than any of those around me.'

'Perhaps you do,' said the Emperor, 'for experience does not always mean wisdom. But time is precious just now, so let us quickly make preparations to start upon our journey.'

The Emperor called his Lord High Chancellor and instructed him how to run the kingdom during his absence. Meanwhile the Scarecrow was taken apart, and the painted sack that served him for a head was carefully laundered and restuffed with the brains originally given him by the great Wizard. His clothes were also cleaned and pressed by the imperial tailors, and his crown polished and again sewed upon his head, for the Tin Woodman insisted he should not renounce this badge of royalty. The Scarecrow now presented a very respectable appearance; and although in no way addicted to vanity, he was quite pleased with himself and strutted a trifle as he walked. While this was being done, Tip mended the wooden limbs of Jack Pumpkinhead and made them stronger than before, and the Sawhorse was also inspected to see if he was in good working order.

Then, bright and early the next morning, they set out upon the return journey to the Emerald City, the Tin Woodman bearing on his shoulder a gleaming axe and leading the way, while the Pumpkinhead rode on the Sawhorse, and Tip and the Scarecrow walked on either side to make sure that he didn't fall off or become damaged.

12.

Mr. H. M. Wogglebug, T.E.

NOW GENERAL JINJUR—who, you will remember, commanded the Army of Revolt—was rendered very uneasy by the escape of the Scarecrow from the Emerald City. She feared, and with good reason, that if His Majesty and the Tin Woodman joined forces, it would mean danger to her and her entire army, for the people of Oz had not yet forgotten the deeds of these famous heroes who had passed successfully through so many startling adventures.

So Jinjur sent post-haste for old Mombi the Witch, and promised her large rewards if she would come to the assistance of the Rebel Army.

Mombi was furious at the trick Tip had played on her—at his escape and the theft of the precious Powder of Life. So she needed no urging to get her to travel to the Emerald City and assist Jinjur in defeating the Scarecrow and the Tin Woodman, who had made Tip one of their friends.

Mombi had no sooner arrived at the royal palace than she discovered, by means of her secret magic, that the adventurers were starting upon their journey to the Emerald City; so she retired to a small room high up in a tower and locked herself in while she practised such magic arts as she could command to prevent the return of the Scarecrow and his friends.

That was why the Tin Woodman presently said:

'Something very curious has happened. I ought to know by heart every step of this journey, and yet I fear we have already lost our way.'

'That is quite impossible!' protested the Scarecrow. 'Why do you think, my dear friend, that we have gone astray?'

'Well, here before us is a great field of sunflowers—and I never saw this field before in all my life.'

At these words they all looked around, only to find that they were indeed surounded by a field of tall stalks, every stalk bearing at its top a gigantic sunflower. And not only were these flowers almost blinding in their vivid hues of red and gold, but each one whirled around on its stalk like a miniature windmill, completely dazzling the vision of the beholders and so mystifying them that they knew not which way to turn. 'It's witchcraft!' exclaimed Tip.

While they paused, hesitating and wondering, the Tin Woodman uttered a cry of impatience and advanced with swinging axe to cut down the stalks before him. But now the sunflowers suddenly stopped their rapid whirling and the travellers plainly saw a girl's face appear in the centre of each flower. These lovely faces looked on the astonished band with mocking smiles, and then burst into a chorus of merry laughter at the dismay their appearance caused.

'Stop! Stop!' cried Tip, seizing the Woodman's arm. 'They're alive! They're girls!'

At that moment the flowers began whirling again, and the faces faded away.

The Tin Woodman dropped his axe and sat down upon the ground.

'It would be heartless to chop down those pretty creatures,' said he despondently, 'and yet I do not know how else we can proceed upon our way.'

'They looked to me strangely like the faces of the Army of Revolt,' mused the Scarecrow. 'But I cannot conceive how the girls could have followed us here.'

'I believe it's magic,' said Tip positively, 'and that some-one is playing a trick on us. I've known old Mombi to do things like that before. Probably it's nothing more than an illusion, and there are no sunflowers here at all.'

'Then let us shut our eyes and walk forward,' suggested the Woodman.

'Excuse me,' replied the Scarecrow. 'My eyes are not painted to shut. Because you happen to have tin eyelids, you must not imagine we are all built in the same way.'

'And the eyes of the Sawhorse are knot eyes,' said Jack, leaning forward to examine them.

'Nevertheless, you must ride quickly forward,' commanded Tip, 'and we will follow after you and so try to escape. My eyes are already dazzled.'

So the Pumpkinhead rode boldly forward, and Tip grasped the stub tail of the Sawhorse and followed with closed eyes. The Scarecrow and the Tin Woodman brought up the rear, and before they had gone many yards a joyful shout from Jack announced that the way was clear before them.

Then all paused to look backward, but not a trace of the field of sunflowers remained.

More cheerfully now, they proceeded upon their journey; but old Mombi had so changed the appearance of the landscape that they would surely have been lost had not the Scarecrow wisely concluded to take their direction from the sun. For no witchcraft could change the course of the sun, and it was therefore a safe guide.

However, other difficulties lay before them. The Sawhorse stepped into a rabbit hole and fell to the ground. The Pumpkinhead was pitched high into the air, and his history would probably have ended at that exact moment had not the Tin Woodman skilfully caught the pumpkin as it descended and saved it from injury.

Tip soon had it fitted to the neck again and replaced Jack upon his feet. But the Sawhorse did not escape so easily. For when his leg was pulled from the rabbit hole, it was found to be broken off short, and must be replaced or repaired before he could go a step farther.

'This is quite serious,' said the Tin Woodman.'If there were trees near by I might soon manufacture another leg for this animal, but I cannot see a tree.'

'And there are neither fences nor houses in this part of the Land of Oz,' added the Scarecrow sadly.

'Then what shall we do?' inquired the boy.

'I suppose I must start my brains working,' replied His Majesty the Scarecrow, 'for experience has taught me that I can do anything if I only take time to think.'

'Let us all think,' said Tip, 'and perhaps we shall find a way to repair the Sawhorse.'

So they sat in a row upon the grass and began to think, while the Sawhorse occupied itself gazing curiously upon its broken limb.

'Does it hurt?' asked the Tin Woodman in a soft, sympathetic voice.

'Not in the least,' returned the Sawhorse, 'but my pride is injured to find that my anatomy is so brittle.'

For a time the little group remained in silent thought. Presently the Tin Woodman raised his head and looked over the fields.

'What sort of creature is that which approaches us?' he asked wonderingly.

The others followed his gaze and discovered coming towards them the most extraordinary object they had ever beheld. It advanced quickly and noiselessly over the soft grass, and in a few minutes stood before the adventurers and regarded them with an astonishment equal to their own.

The Scarecrow was calm under all circumstances.

'Good morning!' he said politely.

The stranger removed his hat with a flourish, bowed very low, and then spoke:

'Good morning, one and all. I hope you are, as an aggregation, enjoying excellent health. Permit me to present my card.'

With this courteous speech it extended a card towards the Scarecrow, who accepted it, turned it over and over, and then handed it with a shake of his head to Tip. The boy read aloud:

MR. H. M. WOGGLEBUG, T.E.

'Dear me!' ejaculated the Pumpkinhead, staring somewhat intently.

'How very peculiar!' said the Tin Woodman.

Tip's eyes were round and wondering, and the Sawhorse uttered a sigh and turned away its head.

'Are you really a Wogglebug?' inquired the Scarecrow.

'Most certainly, my dear sir!' answered the stranger, briskly. 'Is not my name upon the card?'

'It is,' said the Scarecrow. 'But may I ask what "H. M." stands for?'

'H. M. means "Highly Magnified,"' returned the Wogglebug proudly.

'Oh, I see.' The Scarecrow viewed the stranger critically. 'And are you really highly magnified?'

'Sir,' said the Wogglebug, 'I take you for a gentleman of judgment. Does it not occur to you that I am several thousand times greater than any Wogglebug you ever saw before? Therefore it is plainly evident that I am Highly Magnified, and there is no good reason why you should doubt the fact.'

'Pardon me,' returned the Scarecrow. 'My brains are slightly mixed since I was last laundered. Would it be improper for me to ask also what the "T.E." at the end of your name stands for?'

'Those letters express my degree,' answered the Wogglebug with a condescending smile. 'To be more explicit, the initials mean that I am "Thoroughly Educated." '

'Oh!' said the Scarecrow, much relieved.

Tip had not yet taken his eyes off this wonderful personage. What he saw was a great, round buglike body supported upon two slender legs which ended in delicate feet, the toes curling upward. The body of the Wogglebug was rather flat and, judging from what could be seen of it, was of a glistening dark-brown colour upon the back, while the front was striped with alternate bands of light brown and white, blending together at the edges. Its arms were fully as slender as its legs, and upon a rather long neck was perched its head—not unlike the head of a man, except that its nose ended in a curling antenna, or 'feeler', and its ears from the upper points bore antennae that decorated the sides of its head like two miniature curling pig tails. It must be admitted that the round, black eyes were rather bulging in appearance, but the expression upon the Wogglebug's face was by no means unpleasant.

For dress, the insect wore a dark-blue swallowtail coat with a yellow-silk lining and a flower in the buttonhole; a vest of white duck that stretched tightly across the wide body; knickerbockers of fawn-coloured plush, fastened at the knees with gilt buckles; and perched upon its small head, was jauntily set a tall silk hat.

Standing upright before our amazed friends the Wogglebug appeared to be fully as tall as the Tin Woodman, and surely no bug in all the Land of Oz had ever before attained so enormous a size.

'I confess,' said the Scarecrow, 'that your abrupt appearance has caused me surprise, and no doubt has startled my companions. I hope, however, that this circumstance will not distress you. We shall probably get used to you in time.'

'Do not apologize, I beg of you!' returned the Wogglebug earnestly. 'It affords me great pleasure to surprise people; for surely I cannot be classed with ordinary insects, and am entitled to both curiosity and admiration from those I meet.'

'You are indeed,' agreed His Majesty.

'If you will permit me to seat myself in your august company,' continued the stranger, 'I will gladly relate my history, so that you will be better able to comprehend my unusual—may I say remarkable?—appearance.'

'You may say what you please,' answered the Tin Woodman briefly.

So the Wogglebug sat down upon the grass, facing the little group of wanderers, and told them the following story.

13.

A Highly Magnified History

'IT IS BUT HONEST that I should acknowledge at the beginning of my recital that I was born an ordinary Wogglebug,' began the creature, in a frank and friendly tone. 'Knowing no better, I used my arms as well as my legs for walking, and crawled under the edges of stones or hid among the roots of grasses with no thought beyond finding a few insects smaller than myself to feed upon.

'The chill nights rendered me stiff and motionless, for I wore no clothing, but each morning the warm rays of the sun gave me new life and restored me to activity. A horrible existence is this, but you must remember it is the regularly ordained existence of Wogglebugs, as well as of many other tiny creatures that inhabit the earth.

'But destiny had singled me out, humble though I was, for a grander fate! One day I crawled near to a country school-house, and my curiosity being excited by the monotonous hum of the students within, I made bold to enter and creep along a crack between two boards until I reached the far end, where, in front of a hearth of glowing embers, sat the master at his desk.

'No one noticed so small a creature as a Wogglebug, and when I found that the hearth was even warmer and more comfortable than the sunshine, I resolved to establish my future home beside it. So I found a charming nest between two bricks and hid myself therein for many, many months.

'Professor Nowitall is doubtless the most famous scholar in the Land of Oz, and after a few days I began to listen to the lectures and discourses he gave his pupils. Not one of them was more attentive than the humble, unnoticed Wogglebug, and I acquired in this way a fund of knowledge that I will myself confess is simply marvellous. That is why I place T.E.—Thoroughly Educated—upon my cards, for my greatest pride lies in the fact that the world cannot produce another Wogglebug with a tenth part of my own culture and erudition.'

'I do not blame you,' said the Scarecrow. 'Education is a thing to be proud of. I'm educated myself. The mess of brains given me by the Great Wizard is considered by my friends to be unexcelled.'

'Nevertheless,' interrupted the Tin Woodman, 'a good heart is, I believe, much more desirable than education or brains.'

'To me,' said the Sawhorse, 'a good leg is more desirable than either.'

'Could seeds be considered in the light of brains?' inquired the Pumpkinhead abruptly.

'Keep quiet!' commanded Tip sternly.

'Very well, dear Father,' answered the obedient Jack.

The Wogglebug listened patiently—even respectfully

—to these remarks, and then resumed his story:

'I must have lived fully three years in that secluded school-house hearth,' said he, 'drinking thirstily of the ever-flowing fount of limpid knowledge before me.'

'Quite poetical,' commented the Scarecrow, nodding his head approvingly.

'But one day,' continued the Bug, 'a marvellous circumstance occurred that altered my very existence and brought me to my present pinnacle of greatness. The Professor discovered me in the act of crawling across the hearth, and before I could escape he had caught me between his thumb and forefinger.

'"My dear children," said he, "I have captured a Wogglebug—a very rare and interesting specimen. Do any of you know what a Wogglebug is?"

'"No!" yelled the scholars, in chorus.

'"Then," said the Professor, "I will get out my famous magnifying glass and throw the insect upon a screen in a highly magnified condition, that you may all study carefully its peculiar construction and become acquainted with its habits and manner of life."

'He then brought from a cupboard a most curious instrument; and before I could realize what had happened, I found myself thrown upon a screen in a highly magnified state—even as you now behold me.

'The students stood up on their stools and craned their heads forward to get a better view of me, and two little girls jumped upon the sill of an open window where they could see more plainly.

'"Behold!" cried the Professor in a loud voice, "this

highly magnified Wogglebug, one of the most curious insects in existence!"

'Being thoroughly educated, and knowing what is required of a cultured gentleman, at this juncture I stood upright and, placing my hand upon my bosom, made a very polite bow. My action, being unexpected, must have startled them, for one of the little girls perched upon the window sill gave a scream and fell backward out of the window, drawing her companion with her as she disappeared.

'The Professor uttered a cry of horror and rushed away through the door to see if the poor children were injured by the fall. The scholars followed after him in a wild mob, and I was left alone in the schoolroom, still in a highly magnified state and free to do as I pleased.

'It immediately occurred to me that this was a good opportunity to escape. I was proud of my great size, and realized that now I could safely travel anywhere in the world, while my superior culture would make me a fit associate for the most learned person I might chance to meet.

'So, while the Professor picked the little girls—who were more frightened than hurt—off the ground, and the pupils clustered around him closely grouped, I calmly walked out of the school-house, turned a corner, and escaped unnoticed to a grove of trees that stood near.'

'Wonderful!' exclaimed the Pumpkinhead.

'It was indeed,' agreed the Wogglebug. 'I have never ceased to congratulate myself for escaping while I was highly magnified, for even my excessive knowledge would have proved of little use to me had I remained a tiny, insignificant insect.'

'I didn't know before,' said Tip, looking at the Wogglebug with a puzzled expression, 'that insects wore clothes.'

'Nor do they, in their natural state,' returned the stranger. 'But in the course of my wanderings I had the good fortune to save the ninth life of a tailor—tailors having, like cats, nine lives, as you probably know. The fellow was exceedingly grateful, for had he lost that ninth life it would have been the end of him; so he begged permission to furnish me with the stylish costume I now wear. It fits very nicely, does it not?' and the Wogglebug stood up and turned himself around slowly, that all might examine his person.

'He must have been a good tailor,' said the Scarecrow, somewhat enviously.

'He was a good-hearted tailor, at any rate,' observed Nick Chopper.

'But where were you going when you met us?' Tip asked the Wogglebug.

'Nowhere in particular,' was the reply, 'although it is my intention soon to visit the Emerald City and arrange to give a course of lectures to select audiences on the "Advantages of Magnification."'

'We are bound for the Emerald City now,' said the Tin Woodman; 'so, if it pleases you to do so, you are welcome to travel in our company.'

The Wogglebug bowed with profound grace.

'It will give me great pleasure,' said he, to accept your kind invitation, for nowhere in the Land of Oz could I hope to meet with so congenial a company.'

'That is true,' acknowledged the Pumpkinhead. 'We are quite as congenial as flies and honey.'

'But—pardon me if I seem inquisitive—are you not all rather—ahem!—rather unusual?' asked the Wogglebug, looking from one to another with unconcealed interest.

'Not more so than yourself,' answered the Scarecrow. 'Everything in life is unusual until you get accustomed to it.'

'What rare philosophy!' exclaimed the Wogglebug, admiringly.

'Yes; my brains are working well today,' admitted the Scarecrow, an accent of pride in his voice.

'Then, if you are sufficiently rested and refreshed, let us bend our steps towards the Emerald City,' suggested the magnified one.

'We can't,' said Tip. 'The Sawhorse has broken a leg, so he can't bend his steps. And there is no wood around to make him a new limb from. And we can't leave the horse behind because the Pumpkinhead is so stiff in his joints that he has to ride.'

'How very unfortunate!' cried the Wogglebug. Then he looked the party over carefully and said:

'If the Pumpkinhead is to ride, why not use one of his legs to make a leg for the horse that carries him? I judge that both are made of wood.'

'Now that is what I call real cleverness,' said the Scarecrow approvingly. 'I wonder my brains did not think of that long ago! Get to work, my dear Nick, and fit the

Pumpkinhead's leg to the Sawhorse.'

Jack was not especially pleased with this idea; but he submitted to having his left leg amputated by the Tin Woodman and whittled down to fit the left leg of the Sawhorse. Nor was the Sawhorse especially pleased with the operation, either; for he growled a good deal about being 'butchered', as he called it, and afterwards declared that the new leg was a disgrace to a respectable Sawhorse.

'I beg you to be more careful in your speech,' said the Pumpkinhead, sharply. 'Remember, if you please, that it is my leg you are abusing.'

'I cannot forget it,' retorted the Sawhorse, 'for it is quite as flimsy as the rest of your person.'

'Flimsy! Me flimsy!' cried Jack in a rage. 'How dare you call me flimsy?'

'Because you are built as absurdly as a jumping-jack,' sneered the horse, rolling his knotty eyes in a vicious manner. 'Even your head won't stay straight, and you never can tell whether you are looking backward or forward!'

'Friends, I entreat you not to quarrel!' pleaded the Tin Woodman anxiously. 'As a matter of fact, we are none of us above criticism; so let us bear with each other's faults.'

'An excellent suggestion,' said the Wogglebug, approvingly. 'You must have an excellent heart, my metallic friend.'

'I have,' returned Nick, well pleased. 'My heart is quite the best part of me. But now let us start upon our journey.'

They perched the one-legged Pumpkinhead upon the

Sawhorse, and tied him to his seat with cords, so that he could not possibly fall off.

And then, following the lead of the Scarecrow, they advanced in the direction of the Emerald City.

14.

Old Mombi Indulges in Witchcraft

THEY SOON DISCOVERED that the Sawhorse limped, for his new leg was a trifle too long. So they were obliged to halt while the Tin Woodman chopped it down with his axe, after which the wooden steed paced along more comfortably. But the Sawhorse was not entirely satisfied, even yet.

'It was a shame that I broke my other leg!' it growled.

'On the contrary,' airily remarked the Wogglebug, who was walking alongside, 'you should consider the accident most fortunate. For a horse is never of much use until he has been broken.'

'I beg your pardon,' said Tip, rather provoked, for he felt a warm interest in both the Sawhorse and his man Jack, 'but permit me to say that your joke is as old as it is poor.'

'Still, it is a joke,' declared the Wogglebug, firmly, 'and a joke derived from a play on words is considered among educated people to be eminently proper.'

'What does that mean?' inquired the Pumpkinhead.

'It means, my dear friend,' explained the Wogglebug,

'that our language contains many words having a double meaning; and that to pronounce a joke that allows both meanings of a certain word proves the joker a person of culture and refinement, who has, moreover, a thorough command of the language.'

'I don't believe that,' said Tip plainly. 'Anybody can make a pun.'

'Not so,' rejoined the Wogglebug stiffly. 'It requires education of a high order. Are you educated, young sir?'

'Not especially,' admitted Tip.

'Then you cannot judge the matter. I myself am thoroughly educated, and I say that puns display genius. For instance, were I to ride on this Sawhorse, he would not only be an animal—he would then be a horse and buggy.'

At this the Scarecrow gave a gasp and the Tin Woodman stopped short and looked reproachfully at the Wogglebug. At the same time the Sawhorse snorted loudly in derision; and even the Pumpkinhead put up his hand to hide the smile which, because it was carved upon his face, he could not change to a frown.

But the Wogglebug strutted along as if he had made some brilliant remark, and the Scarecrow was obliged to say:

'I have heard, my dear friend, that a person can become overeducated; and although I have a high respect for brains, no matter how they may be arranged or classified, I begin to suspect that yours are slightly tangled. In any event, I must beg you to restrain your superior education while in our society.'

'We are not very particular,' added the Tin Woodman, 'and we are exceedingly kindhearted. But if your superior culture gets leaky again——' He did not complete the sentence, but he twirled his gleaming axe so carelessly that the Wogglebug looked frightened and shrank away to a safe distance.

The others marched on in silence, and the highly magnified one, after a period of deep thought, said in a humble voice :

'I will endeavour to restrain myself.'

'That is all we can expect,' returned the Scarecrow pleasantly; and good nature being thus happily restored to the party, they proceeded on their way.

When they again stopped to allow Tip to rest—the boy being the only one that seemed to tire—the Tin Woodman noticed many small, round holes in the grassy meadow.

'This must be a village of the field mice,' he said to the Scarecrow. 'I wonder if my old friend the Queen of the Mice is in this neighbourhood.'

'If she is, she may be of great service to us,' answered the Scarecrow, who was impressed by a sudden thought. 'See if you can call her, my dear Nick.'

So the Tin Woodman blew a shrill note upon a silver whistle that hung around his neck, and presently a tiny grey mouse popped from a nearby hole and advanced fearlessly towards them. For the Tin Woodman had once saved her life, and the Queen of the Field Mice knew he was to be trusted.

'Good day, your Majesty,' said Nick, politely addressing

the Mouse; 'I trust you are enjoying good health?'

'Thank you, I am quite well,' answered the Queen demurely, as she sat up and displayed the tiny golden crown
upon her head. 'Can I do anything to assist my old friends?'

'You can indeed,' replied the Scarecrow eagerly. 'Let
me, I entreat you, take a dozen of your subjects with me
to the Emerald City.'

'Will they be injured in any way?' asked the Queen
doubtfully.

'I think not,' replied the Scarecrow. 'I will carry them
hidden in the straw which stuffs my body, and when I give
them the signal by unbuttoning my jacket, they have only
to rush out and scamper home again as fast as they can.
By doing this they will assist me to regain my throne,
which the Army of Revolt has taken from me.'

'In that case,' said the Queen, 'I will not refuse your
request. Whenever you are ready, I will call twelve of my
most intelligent subjects.'

'I am ready now,' returned the Scarecrow. Then he lay
flat on the ground and unbuttoned his jacket, displaying
the straw with which he was stuffed.

The Queen uttered a little piping call, and in an instant
a dozen pretty field mice had emerged from their holes and
stood before their ruler, awaiting her orders.

What the Queen said to them none of our travellers
could understand, for it was in the mouse language; but
the field mice obeyed without hesitation, running one
after the other to the Scarecrow and hiding themselves in
the straw of his breast.

When all of the twelve mice had thus concealed themselves, the Scarecrow buttoned his jacket securely and then arose and thanked the Queen.

'One thing more you might do to serve us,' suggested the Tin Woodman, 'and that is to run ahead and show us the way to the Emerald City. For some enemy is trying to prevent us from reaching it.'

'I will do that gladly,' returned the Queen. 'Are you ready?'

The Tin Woodman looked at Tip.

'I'm rested,' said the boy. 'Let us start.'

Then they resumed their journey, the little grey Queen of the Field Mice running swiftly ahead and then pausing until the travellers drew near, when away she would dart again.

Without this unerring guide the Scarecrow and his comrades might never have gained the Emerald City, for many were the obstacles thrown in their way by the arts of old Mombi. Yet not one of the obstacles really existed—all were cleverly contrived deceptions. For when they came to the banks of a rushing river that threatened to bar their way the little Queen kept steadily on, passing through the seeming flood in safety; and our travellers followed her without encountering a single drop of water.

Again, a high wall of granite towered high above their heads and opposed their advance. But the grey Field Mouse walked straight through it, and the others did the same, the wall melting into mist as they passed through it.

Afterwards, when they had stopped for a moment to allow Tip to rest, they saw forty roads branching off from their feet in forty different directions; and soon these forty roads began whirling around like a mighty wheel, first in one direction and then in the other, completely bewildering their vision.

But the Queen called for them to follow her and darted off in a straight line; and when they had gone a few paces the whirling pathways vanished and were seen no more.

Mombi's last trick was most fearful of all. She sent a sheet of crackling flame rushing over the meadow to consume them, and for the first time the Scarecrow became afraid and turned to fly.

'If that fire reaches me, I will be gone in no time!' said he, trembling until his straw rattled. 'It's the most dangerous thing I ever encountered.'

'I'm off, too!' cried the Sawhorse, turning and prancing with agitation; 'for my wood is so dry it would burn like kindlings.'

'Is fire dangerous to pumpkins?' asked Jack fearfully.

'You'll be baked like a tart—and so will I!' answered the Wogglebug, getting down on all fours so he could run the faster.

But the Tin Woodman, having no fear of fire, averted the stampede by a few sensible words.

'Look at the Field Mouse!' he shouted. 'The fire does not burn her in the least. In fact, it is no fire at all, but only a deception.'

Indeed, to watch the little Queen march calmly through the advancing flames restored courage to every member of the party, and they followed her without even being scorched.

'This is surely a most extraordinary adventure,' said the Wogglebug, who was greatly amazed, 'for it upsets all the natural laws that I heard Professor Nowitall teach in the school-house.'

'Of course it does,' said the Scarecrow wisely. 'All magic

is unnatural, and for that reason is to be feared and avoided. But I see before us the gates of the Emerald City, so I imagine we have now overcome all the magical obstacles that seemed to oppose us.'

Indeed, the walls of the city were plainly visible, and the Queen of the Field Mice, who had guided them so faithfully, came near to bid them good-bye.

'We are very grateful to Your Majesty for your kind assistance,' said the Tin Woodman, bowing before the pretty creature.

'I am always pleased to be of service to my friends,' answered the Queen, and in a flash she had darted away upon her journey home.

15.

The Prisoners of
the Queen

APPROACHING THE GATEWAY of the Emerald City, the travellers found it guarded by two girls of the Army of Revolt, who opposed their entrance by drawing the knitting needles from their hair and threatening to prod the first that came near.

But the Tin Woodman was not afraid.

'At the worst they can but scratch my beautiful nickel-plate,' he said. 'But there will be no "worst", for I think I can manage to frighten these absurd soldiers very easily. Follow me closely, all of you!'

Then, swinging his axe in a great circle to right and left before him, he advanced upon the gate, and the others followed him without hesitation.

The girls, who had expected no resistance whatever, were terrified by the sweep of the glittering axe and fled screaming into the city, so that our travellers passed the gates in safety and marched down the green marble pavement of the wide street towards the royal palace.

'At this rate we will soon have Your Majesty upon the

throne again,' said the Tin Woodman, laughing at his easy conquest of the guards.

'Thank you, friend Nick,' returned the Scarecrow. 'Nothing can resist your kind heart and sharp axe.'

As they passed the rows of houses, they saw through the open doors that men were sweeping and dusting and washing dishes, while the women sat around in groups, gossiping and laughing.

'What has happened?' the Scarecrow asked a sad-looking man with a bushy beard, who wore an apron and was wheeling a baby carriage along the sidewalk.

'Why, we've had a revolution, Your Majesty—as you ought to know very well,' replied the man; 'and since you went away, the women have been running things to suit themselves. I'm glad you have decided to come back and restore order, for doing housework and minding the children is wearing out the strength of every man in the Emerald City.'

'Hm!' said the Scarecrow, thoughtfully. 'If it is such hard work as you say, how did the women manage it so easily?'

'I really do not know,' replied the man, with a deep sigh. 'Perhaps the women are made of iron.'

No movement was made, as they passed along the street, to oppose their progress. Several of the women stopped their gossip long enough to cast curious looks upon our friends, but immediately they would turn away with a laugh or a sneer and resume their chatter. And when they met with several girls belonging to the Army of Revolt, those soldiers, instead of being alarmed or appearing

surprised, merely stepped out of the way and allowed them to advance.

This action rendered the Scarecrow uneasy.

'I'm afraid we are walking into a trap,' said he.

'Nonsense!' returned Nick Chopper confidently. 'The silly creatures are conquered already!'

But the Scarecrow shook his head in a way that expressed doubt, and Tip said:

'It's too easy, altogether. Look out for trouble ahead.'

'I will,' returned His Majesty.

Unopposed, they reached the royal palace and marched up the marble steps, which had once been thickly encrusted with emeralds but were now filled with tiny holes where the jewels had been ruthlessly torn from their settings by the Army of Revolt. And so far not a rebel barred their way.

Through the arched hallways and into the magnificent throne room marched the Tin Woodman and his followers, and here, when the green silk curtains fell behind them, they saw a curious sight.

Seated within the glittering throne was General Jinjur, with the Scarecrow's second-best crown upon her head and the royal sceptre in her right hand. A box of caramels, from which she was eating, rested in her lap, and the girl seemed entirely at ease in her royal surroundings.

Th Scarecrow stepped forward and confronted her, while the Tin Woodman leaned upon his axe and the others formed a half-circle back of His Majesty's person.

'How dare you sit on my throne?' demanded the Scarecrow, sternly eyeing the intruder. 'Don't you know you are guilty of treason, and that there is a law against treason?'

'The throne belongs to whoever is able to take it,' answered Jinjur, as she slowly ate another caramel. 'I have taken it, as you see; so just now I am the Queen, and all who oppose me are guilty of treason and must be punished by the law you have just mentioned.'

This view of the case puzzled the Scarecrow.

'How is it, friend Nick?' he asked, turning to the Tin Woodman.

'Why, when it comes to law, I have nothing to say, answered that personage; 'for laws were never meant to be understood, and it is foolish to make the attempt.'

'Then what shall we do?' asked the Scarecrow, in dismay.

'Why don't you marry the Queen? And then you can both rule,' suggested the Wogglebug.

Jinjur glared at the insect fiercely.

'Why don't you send her back to her mother, where she belongs?' asked Jack Pumpkinhead.

Jinjur frowned.

'Why don't you shut her up in a closet until she behaves herself and promises to be good?' inquired Tip.

Jinjur's lip curled scornfully.

'Or give her a good shaking!' added the Sawhorse.

'No,' said the Tin Woodman, 'we must treat the poor girl with gentleness. Let us give her all the jewels she can carry, and send her away happy and contented.'

At this Queen Jinjur laughed aloud, and the next minute clapped her pretty hands together thrice, as if for a signal.

'You are very absurd creatures,' said she, 'but I am tired of your nonsense and have no time to bother with you longer.'

While the monarch and his friends listened in amazement to this impudent speech, a startling thing happened. The Tin Woodman's axe was snatched from his grasp by some person behind him, and he found himself disarmed and helpless. At the same instant a shout of laughter rang in the ears of the devoted band, and turning to see whence this came they found themselves surrounded by the Army of Revolt, the girls bearing in either hand their glistening knitting needles. The entire throne room seemed to be filled with the rebels, and the Scarecrow and his comrades realized that they were prisoners.

'You see how foolish it is to oppose a woman's wit,' said Jinjur gaily; 'and this event only proves that I am more fit to rule the Emerald City than a Scarecrow. I bear you no ill will, I assure you; but lest you should prove troublesome to me in the future I shall order you all to be destroyed. That is, all except the boy, who belongs to old Mombi and must be restored to her keeping. The rest of you are not human, and therefore it will not be wicked to demolish you. The Sawhorse and the Pumpkinhead's body I will have chopped up for kindling wood, and the pumpkin shall be made into tarts. The Scarecrow will do nicely to start a bonfire; the Tin Woodman can be cut into small pieces and fed to the goats. As for this Wogglebug—'

'Highly Magnified, if you please!' interrupted the insect.

'I think I will ask the cook to make green-turtle soup of

you,' continued the Queen, reflectively.

The Wogglebug shuddered.

'Or, if that won't do, we might use you for a Hungarian goulash, stewed and highly spiced,' she added, cruelly.

This programme of extermination was so terrible that the prisoners looked upon one another in a panic of fear. The Scarecrow alone did not give way to despair. He stood quietly before the Queen, and his brow was wrinkled in deep thought as he strove to find some means to escape.

While thus engaged, he felt the straw within his breast move gently. At once his expression changed from sadness to joy, and raising his hand he quickly unbuttoned the front of his jacket.

This action did not pass unnoticed by the crowd of girls clustered about him, but none of them suspected what he was doing until a tiny grey mouse leaped from his bosom to the floor and scampered away between the feet of the Army of Revolt. Another mouse quickly followed; then another and another, in rapid succession. And suddenly such a scream of terror went up from the Army that it might easily have filled the stoutest heart with consternation. The flight that ensued turned to a stampede, and the stampede to a panic.

For while the startled mice rushed wildly about the room, the Scarecrow had only time to note a whirl of skirts and a twinkling of feet as the girls disappeared from the palace—pushing and crowding one another in their mad efforts to escape.

The Queen, at the first alarm, stood up on the cushions of the throne and began to dance frantically upon her tiptoes. Then a mouse ran up the cushions, and with a terrified leap poor Jinjur shot clear over the head of the Scarecrow and escaped through an archway—never pausing in her wild career until she had reached the city gates.

So, in less time than I can explain, the throne room was deserted by all save the Scarecrow and his friends, and the Wogglebug heaved a deep sigh of relief as he exclaimed, 'Thank goodness, we are saved!'

'For a time, yes,' answered the Tin Woodman. 'But the enemy will soon return, I fear.' He picked up his axe from the floor where a fleeing soldier had dropped it.

'Let us bar all the entrances to the palace!' said the Scarecrow. 'Then we shall have time to think what is best to be done.'

So all except Jack Pumpkinhead, who was still tied fast to the Sawhorse, ran to the various doors, bolting and locking them securely. Then, knowing that the Army of Revolt could not batter down the barriers in several days, the adventurers gathered once more in the throne room for a council of war.

16.

The Scarecrow Takes Time to Think

'IT SEEMS TO ME,' began the Scarecrow, when all were again assembled in the throne room, 'that the girl Jinjur is quite right in claiming to be Queen. And if she is right, then I am wrong, and we have no business to be occupying her palace.'

'But you were King until she came,' said the Wogglebug, strutting up and down with his hands in his pockets; 'so it appears to me that she is the interloper instead of you.'

'Especially as we have just conquered her and put her to flight,' added the Pumpkinhead, as he raised his hands to turn his face towards the Scarecrow.

'Have we really conquered her?' asked the Scarecrow, quietly. 'Look out of the window, and tell me what you see.'

Tip ran to the window and looked out.

'The palace is surrounded by a double row of girl soldiers,' he announced.

'I thought so,' returned the Scarecrow. 'We are as truly their prisoners as we were before the mice frightened them from the palace.'

'My friend is right,' said Nick Chopper, who had been polishing his breast with a bit of chamois leather. 'Jinjur is still Queen, and we are prisoners.'

'But I hope she cannot get at us,' exclaimed the Pumpkinhead, with a shiver of fear. 'She threatened to make tarts of me, you know.'

'Don't worry,' said the Tin Woodman. 'It cannot matter greatly. If you stay shut up here you will spoil in time, anyway. A good tart is far more admirable than a decayed intellect.'

'Very true,' agreed the Scarecrow.

'Oh, dear!' moaned Jack; 'what an unhappy lot is mine! Why, dear Father, did you not make me out of tin—or even out of straw—so that I would keep indefinitely?'

'Shucks!' returned Tip indignantly. 'You ought to be glad that I made you at all.' Then he added, reflectively, 'Everything has to come to an end.'

'But I beg to remind you,' broke in the Wogglebug, who had a distressed look in his bulging, round eyes, 'that this terrible Queen Jinjur suggested making a goulash of me—*Me!* the only Highly Magnified and Thoroughly Educated Wogglebug in the wide, wide world!'

'I think it was a brilliant idea,' remarked the Scarecrow approvingly.

'Don't you imagine he would make a better soup?' asked the Tin Woodman, turning towards his friend.

'Well, perhaps,' acknowledged the Scarecrow.

The Wogglebug groaned.

'I can see, in my mind's eye,' said he, mournfully, 'the

goats eating small pieces of my dear comrade, the Tin Woodman, while my soup is being cooked on a bonfire built of the Sawhorse and Jack Pumpkinhead's body, and Queen Jinjur watches me boil while she feeds the flames with my friend the Scarecrow!'

This morbid picture cast a gloom over the entire party, making them restless and anxious.

'It can't happen for some time,' said the Tin Woodman, trying to speak cheerfully, 'for we shall be able to keep Jinjur out of the palace until she manages to break down the doors.'

'And in the meantime I am liable to starve to death, and so is the Wogglebug,' announced Tip.

'As for me,' said the Wogglebug. 'I think that I could live for some time on Jack Pumpkinhead. Not that I prefer pumpkins for food; but I believe they are somewhat nutritious, and Jack's head is large and plump.'

'How heartless!' exclaimed the Tin Woodman, greatly shocked. 'Are we cannibals, let me ask? Or are we faithful friends?'

'I see very clearly that we cannot stay shut up in this palace,' said the Scarecrow with decision. 'So let us end this mournful talk and try to discover a means to escape.'

At this suggstion they all gathered eagerly around the throne, wherein was seated the Scarecrow; and as Tip sat down upon a stool, there fell from his pocket a pepper-box, which rolled upon the floor.

'What is this?' asked Nick Chopper, picking up the box.

'Be careful!' cried the boy. 'That's my Powder of Life. Don't spill it, for it is nearly gone.'

'And what is the Powder of Life?' inquired the Scarecrow, as Tip replaced the box carefully in his pocket.

'It's some magical stuff old Mombi got from a crooked Sorcerer,' explained the boy. 'She brought Jack to life with it, and afterwards I used it to bring the Sawhorse to life. I guess it will make anything live that is sprinkled with it; but there's only about one dose left.'

'Then it is very precious,' said the Tin Woodman.

'Indeed it is,' agreed the Scarecrow. 'It may prove our best means of escape from our difficulties. I believe I will think for a few minutes, so I will thank you, friend Tip, to get out your knife and rip this heavy crown from my forehead.'

Tip soon cut the stitches that had fastened the crown to the Scarecrow's head, and the former monarch of the Emerald City removed it with a sigh of relief and hung it on a peg beside the throne.

'That is my last memento of royalty,' said he, 'and I'm glad to get rid of it. The former King of this city, who was named Pastoria, lost the crown to the Wonderful Wizard, who passed it on to me. Now the girl Jinjur claims it, and I sincerely hope it will not give her a headache.'

'A kindly thought, which I greatly admire,' said the Tin Woodman, nodding approvingly.

'And now I will indulge in a quiet think,' continued the Scarecrow, lying back in the throne.

The others remained as silent and still as possible, so as not to disturb him; for all had great confidence in the extraordinary brains of the Scarecrow.

And, after what seemed a very long time indeed to the anxious watchers, the thinker sat up, looked upon his friends with a whimsical expression, and said:

'My brains work beautifully today. I'm quite proud of them. Now listen! If we attempt to escape through the doors of the palace, we shall surely be captured. And, as we can't escape through the ground, there is only one other thing to be done: we must escape through the air!'

He paused to note the effect of these words, but all his hearers seemed puzzled and unconvinced.

'The Wonderful Wizard escaped in a balloon,' he continued. 'We don't know how to make a balloon, of course; but any sort of thing that can fly through the air can carry us easily. So I suggest that my friend the Tin Woodman, who is a skilful mechanic, shall build some sort of machine, with good strong wings, to carry us; and our friend Tip can then bring the Thing to life with his magical powder.'

'Bravo!' cried Nick Chopper.

'What splendid brains!' murmured Jack.

'Really quite clever!' said the thoroughly educated Wogglebug.

'I believe it can be done,' declared Tip; 'that is, if the Tin Woodman is equal to making the thing.'

'I'll do my best,' said Nick cheerily; 'and, as a matter of fact, I do not often fail in what I attempt. But the thing will have to be built on the roof of the palace, so it can rise comfortably into the air.'

'To be sure,' said the Scarecrow.

'Then let us search through the palace,' continued the Tin Woodman, 'and carry all the material we can find to the roof, where I will begin my work.'

'First, however,' said the Pumpkinhead, 'I beg you to release me from this horse and make me another leg to walk with. For in my present condition I am of no use to myself or to anyone else.'

So the Tin Woodman knocked a mahogany centre table to pieces with his axe and fitted one of the legs, which was beautifully carved, on to the body of Jack Pumpkinhead, who was very proud of his new limb.

'It seems strange,' said he, as he watched the Tin Woodman work, 'that my left leg should be the most elegant and substantial part of me.'

'That proves you are unusual,' returned the Scarecrow, 'and I am convinced that the only people worthy of consideration in this world are the unusual ones. For the common folk are like the leaves of a tree, and live and die unnoticed.'

'Spoken like a philosopher!' cried the Wogglebug, as he assisted the Tin Woodman to set Jack upon his feet.

'How do you feel now?' asked Tip, watching the Pumpkinhead stump around to try his new leg.

'As good as new,' answered Jack joyfully, 'and quite ready to assist you all to escape.'

'Then let us get to work,' said the Scarecrow, in a businesslike tone.

So, glad to be doing anything that might lead to the end of their captivity, the friends separated to wander over the palace in search of fitting material to use in the construction of their aerial machine.

17.

The Astonishing Flight
of the Gump

WHEN THE ADVENTURERS REASSEMBLED upon the roof, it
was found that a remarkably queer assortment of articles
had been selected by the various members of the party.
No one seemed to have a very clear idea of what was required, but all had brought something.

The Wogglebug had taken from its position over the
mantelpiece in the great hallway the head of a Gump,
which was adorned with wide-spreading antlers; and this,
with great care and greater difficulty, the insect had carried
up the stairs to the roof. This Gump resembled an elk's
head, only the nose turned upward in a saucy manner and
there were whiskers upon its chin, like those of a billy-
goat.

Tip, with the aid of the Sawhorse, had brought a large,
upholstered sofa to the roof. It was an old-fashioned piece
of furniture, with high back and ends, and it was so heavy
that even by resting the greatest weight upon the back of
the Sawhorse, the boy found himself out of breath when
at last the clumsy sofa was dumped on the roof.

The Pumpkinhead had brought a broom, which was

the first thing he saw. The Scarecrow arrived with a coil of clothesline and ropes which he had taken from the courtyard, and in his trip up the stairs he had become so entangled in the loose ends of the ropes that both he and his burden tumbled in a heap upon the roof and might have rolled off if Tip had not rescued him.

The Tin Woodman appeared last. He also had been to the courtyard, where he had cut four great, spreading leaves from a huge palm tree that was the pride of all the inhabitants of the Emerald City.

'My dear Nick!' exclaimed the Scarecrow, seeing what his friend had done, 'you have been guilty of the greatest crime any person can commit in the Emerald City. If I remember rightly, the penalty for chopping leaves from the royal palm tree is to be killed seven times and after-wards imprisoned for life.'

'It cannot be helped now,' answered the Tin Woodman, throwing down the big leaves upon the roof. 'But it may be one more reason why it is necessary for us to escape. And now let us see what you have found for me to work with.'

Many were the doubtful looks they cast upon the heap of materials that now cluttered the roof, and finally the Scarecrow shook his head and remarked:

'Well, if friend Nick can manufacture, from this mess of rubbish, a thing that will fly through the air and carry us to safety, then he is an even better mechanic than I suspected.'

'The first thing required,' said the Tin Woodman, 'is a body big enough to carry the entire party. This sofa is the biggest thing we have, and might be used for a body. But, should the machine ever tip sideways, we would all slide off and fall.'

'Why not use two sofas?' asked Tip. 'There's another one just like this downstairs.'

'That is a very sensible suggestion,' exclaimed the Tin Woodman.

So Tip and the Sawhorse managed, with much labour, to get the second sofa to the roof; and when the two were placed together, edge to edge, the backs and ends formed a protecting wall around the seats.

'Excellent!' cried the Scarecrow. 'We can ride within this snug nest quite at our ease.'

The two sofas were now bound firmly together with

ropes and clothesline, and then Nick Chopper fastened the Gump's head to one end.

'That will show which is the front end of the thing,' said he, greatly pleased with the idea. 'And, really, if you examine it critically, the Gump looks very well as a figure-head. These great palm leaves, for which I have en-dangered my life seven times, must serve us as wings.'

'Are they strong enough?' asked the boy.

'They are as strong as anything we can get,' answered the Woodman; 'although they are small in proportion to the thing's body.'

So he fastened the palm leaves to the sofas, two on each side.

The Wogglebug said in admiration, 'The thing is now complete, and only needs to be brought to life.'

'Stop a moment!' exclaimed Jack. 'Aren't you going to use my broom?'

'What for?' asked the Scarecrow.

'Why, it can be fastened to the back end for a tail,' answered the Pumpkinhead. 'Surely you would not call the thing complete without a tail.'

'Hm!' said the Tin Woodman. 'I do not see the use of a tail. We are not trying to copy a beast, or a fish, or a bird. All we ask of the thing is to carry us through the air.'

'Perhaps, after the thing is brought to life, it can use a tail to steer with,' suggested the Scarecrow. 'For if it flies through the air it will not be unlike a bird, and I've noticed that all birds have tails, which they use for a rudder while they are flying.'

'Very well,' answered Nick, 'the broom shall be used for

a tail,' and he fastened it firmly to the back end of the sofa body.

Tip took the pepper-box from his pocket.

'The thing looks very big,' he said anxiously, 'and I am not sure there is enough powder left to bring all of it to life. But I'll make it go as far as possible.'

'And don't forget the head!' exclaimed the Wogglebug.

'Or the tail!' added Jack Pumpkinhead.

'Do be quiet,' said Tip nervously. 'You must give me a chance to work the magic charm in the proper manner.'

Very carefully, he began sprinkling the thing with the precious powder. Each of the four wings was first lightly covered with a layer; then the sofas were sprinkled, and the broom given a slight coating.

'The head! The head! Don't, I beg of you, forget the head!' cried the Wogglebug, excitedly.

'There's only a little of the powder left,' answered Tip, looking within the box. 'And it seems to me it is more important to bring the legs of the sofas to life than the head.'

'Not so,' decided the Scarecrow. 'Everything must have a head to direct it; and since this creature is to fly, and not walk, it is really unimportant whether its legs are alive or not.'

So Tip sprinkled the Gump's head with the remainder of the powder.

'Now,' said he, 'keep silence while I work the charm!'

Having heard old Mombi pronounce the magic words, and having also succeeded in bringing the Sawhorse to life, Tip did not hesitate an instant in speaking the three cabalistic words, each accompanied by the peculiar gesture of the hands.

It was a grave and impressive ceremony.

As he finished the incantation, the thing shuddered throughout its huge bulk, the Gump gave the screeching cry that is familiar to those animals, and then the four wings began flopping furiously.

Tip managed to grasp a chimney, else he would have been blown off the roof by the terrible breeze raised by the

wings. The Scarecrow, being light in weight, was caught up bodily and borne through the air, until Tip luckily seized him by one leg and held him fast. The Wogglebug lay flat on the roof, and so escaped harm; and the Tin Woodman, whose weight of tin anchored him firmly, threw both arms around Jack Pumpkinhead and managed to save him. The Sawhorse toppled over upon his back and lay with his legs waving helplessly above him.

And now, while all were struggling to recover themselves, the thing rose slowly into the air.

'Here! Come back!' cried Tip, in a frightened voice, as he clung to the chimney with one hand and the Scarecrow with the other. 'Come back at once!'

It was now that the wisdom of the Scarecrow, in bringing the head of the thing to life instead of the legs, was proved beyond a doubt. For the Gump, already high in the air, turned its head at Tip's command and gradually circled around until it could view the roof of the palace.

'Come back!' shouted the boy again.

And the Gump obeyed, slowly and gracefully waving its four wings in the air until it had settled down quietly on the roof once more.

18.

In the Jackdaws' Nest

'THIS,' SAID THE GUMP, in a squeaky voice not at all in keeping with its great body, 'is the most novel experience I ever heard of. The last thing I remember is walking through the forest and hearing a loud noise. Something probably killed me then, and it certainly ought to have been the end of me. Yet here I am, alive again, with four monstrous wings and a body which would make any respectable animal or fowl weep with shame to own. What does it all mean? Am I a Gump, or not?'

'You're just a thing,' answered Tip, 'with a Gump's head on it. And we have made you and brought you to life so that you may carry us through the air wherever we wish to go.'

'Very good!' said the thing. 'As I am not a real Gump, I cannot have a Gump's pride or independent spirit. So I may as well become your servant as anything else. My only satisfaction is that I do not seem to have a very strong constitution and am not likely to live long in a state of slavery.'

'Don't say that, I beg of you!' cried the Tin Woodman, whose excellent heart was strongly affected by this sad speech. 'Are you not feeling well today?'

'Oh, as for that,' returned the Gump, 'it is my first day of existence, so I cannot judge whether I am feeling well or ill.' And it waved its broom tail to and fro in a pensive manner.

'Come, come!' said the Scarecrow kindly. 'Do try to be more cheerful and take life as you find it. We shall be kind masters, and will strive to render your existence as pleasant as possible. Are you willing to carry us through the air wherever we wish to go?'

'Certainly,' answered the Gump. 'I greatly prefer to navigate the air. For should I travel on the earth and meet with one of my own species, my embarrassment would be something awful!'

'I can appreciate that,' said the Tin Woodman sympathetically.

'And yet,' continued the thing, 'when I carefully look you over, my masters, none of you seems to be constructed much more artistically than I am.'

'Appearances are deceitful,' said the Wogglebug earnestly. 'I am both Highly Magnified and Thoroughly Educated.'

'Indeed!' murmured the Gump indifferently.

'And my brains are considered remarkably rare specimens,' added the Scarecrow, proudly.

'How strange!' remarked the Gump.

'Although I am of tin,' said the Woodman, 'I own a heart altogether the warmest in the world.'

'I'm delighted to hear it,' replied the Gump, with a slight cough.

'My smile,' said Jack Pumpkinhead, 'is worthy of your best attention. It is always the same.'

'I am proud indeed to meet with such exceptional masters,' said the Gump, in a careless tone. 'If I could have as complete an introduction to myself, I would be more than satisfied.'

'That will come in time,' remarked the Scarecrow. 'But now,' he added, turning to the others, 'let us get aboard and start upon our journey.'

'Where shall we go?' asked Tip, as he clambered to a seat on the sofas and assisted the Pumpkinhead to follow him.

'In the South Country rules a very delightful Queen called Glinda the Good, who I am sure will gladly receive us,' said the Scarecrow, getting aboard the Gump clumsily. 'Let us go to her and ask her advice.'

'That is a clever thought,' declared Nick Chopper. He gave the Wogglebug a boost and then toppled the Sawhorse into the rear end of the cushioned seats. 'I know Glinda the Good, and believe she will prove a friend indeed.'

'Are we all ready?' asked the boy.

'Yes,' answered the Tin Woodman, seating himself beside the Scarecrow.

'Then,' said Tip, addressing the Gump, 'be kind enough to fly us to the South; and do not go higher than to escape the houses and trees, for it makes me dizzy to be up so far.'

'All right,' answered the Gump briefly.

It flopped its four huge wings and rose slowly into the air; and then, while our little band of adventurers clung to the backs and sides of the sofas for support, the Gump turned towards the south and soared swiftly and majestically away.

'The scenic effect, from this altitude, is marvellous,' commented the educated Wogglebug, as they rode along.

'Never mind the scenery,' said the Scarecrow. 'Hold on tight, or you may tumble out. The Gump seems to rock badly.'

'It will be dark soon,' said Tip, observing that the sun was low on the horizon. 'Perhaps we should have waited until morning. I wonder if the Gump can fly in the night.'

'I've been wondering that myself,' returned the Gump quietly. 'You see, this is a new experience to me. I used to have legs that carried me swiftly over the ground. But now my legs feel asleep.'

'They are,' said Tip. 'We didn't bring 'em to life.'

'You're expected to fly,' explained the Scarecrow, 'not to walk.'

'We can walk ourselves,' said the Wogglebug.

'I begin to understand what is required of me,' remarked the Gump; 'so I will do my best to please you,' and he flew on for a time in silence.

Presently Jack Pumpkinhead became uneasy.

'I wonder if riding through the air is liable to spoil pumpkins?' he said.

'Not unless you carelessly drop your head over the side,' answered the Wogglebug. 'In that event your head would no longer be a pumpkin, for it would become a squash.'

'Haven't I asked you to restrain these unfeeling jokes?' demanded Tip, glaring at the Wogglebug.

'You have; and I've restrained a good many of them,'

replied the insect. 'But there are opportunities for so many excellent puns in our language that, to an educated person like myself, the temptation to express them is almost irresistible.'

'People with more or less education discovered those puns centuries ago,' said Tip.

'Are you sure?' asked the Wogglebug, startled.

'Of course I am,' answered the boy. 'An educated Wogglebug may be a new thing, but a Wogglebug education is as old as the hills.'

The insect seemed much impressed by this remark, and for a time maintained a meek silence.

The Scarecrow, in shifting his seat, saw upon the cushions the pepper-box which Tip had cast aside, and began to examine it.

'Throw it overboard,' said the boy; 'it's quite empty now, and there's no use keeping it.'

'Is it really empty?' asked the Scarecrow, looking curiously into the box.

'Of course it is,' answered Tip. 'I shook out every grain of the powder.'

'Then the box has two bottoms,' announced the Scarecrow; 'for the bottom on the inside is fully an inch away from the bottom on the outside.'

'Let me see,' said the Tin Woodman, taking the box from his friend. 'Yes,' he declared, after looking it over, 'the thing certainly has a false bottom. Now I wonder what that is for?'

'Can't you take it apart and find out?' inquired Tip,

now quite interested in the mystery.

'Why, yes; the lower bottom unscrews,' said the Tin Woodman. 'My fingers are rather stiff; please see if you can open it.'

He handed the pepper-box to Tip, who had no difficulty in unscrewing the bottom. And in the cavity below were three silver pills, with a carefully folded paper lying underneath them.

This paper the boy proceeded to unfold, taking care not to spill the pills, and found several lines clearly written in red ink.

'Read it aloud,' said the Scarecrow, so Tip read as follows:

DR. NIKIDIK'S CELEBRATED WISHING PILLS

Directions for Use: Swallow one pill, count seventeen by twos, then make a wish. The wish will immediately be granted.

CAUTION: Keep in a dry and dark place.

'Why, this is a very valuable discovery!' cried the Scarecrow.

'It is indeed,' replied Tip, gravely. 'These pills may be of great use to us. I wonder if old Mombi knew they were in the bottom of the pepper-box. I remember hearing her say that she got the Powder of Life from this same Nikidik.'

'He must be a powerful Sorcerer!' exclaimed the Tin Woodman; 'and since the powder proved a success, we ought to have confidence in the pills.'

'But how,' asked the Scarecrow, 'can anyone count

seventeen by twos? It is an odd number.'

'That is true,' replied Tip, greatly disappointed. 'No one can possibly count seventeen by twos.'

'Then the pills are of no use to us,' wailed the Pumpkin-head. 'And this fact overwhelms me with grief, for I had intended wishing that my head would never spoil.'

'Nonsense!' said the Scarecrow sharply. 'If we could use the pills at all, we would make far better wishes than that.'

'I do not see how anything could be better,' protested poor Jack. 'If you were liable to spoil at any time, you could understand my anxiety.'

'For my part,' said the Tin Woodman, 'I sympathize with you in every respect. But since we cannot count seventeen by twos, sympathy is all you are liable to get.'

By this time it had become quite dark, and the voyagers found above them a cloudy sky, through which the rays of the moon could not penetrate.

The Gump flew steadily on, and for some reason the huge sofa-body rocked more and more dizzily.

The Wogglebug declared he was seasick, and Tip was also pale and somewhat distressed. But the others clung to the backs of the sofas and did not seem to mind the motion, as long as they were not tipped out.

Darker and darker grew the night, and on and on sped the Gump through the black heavens. The travellers could not see even one another, and an oppressive silence settled down upon them.

After a long time Tip, who had been thinking deeply, spoke.

'How are we to know when we come to the palace of Glinda the Good?' he asked.

'It's a long way to Glinda's palace,' answered the Woodman; 'I've travelled it.'

'But how are we to know how fast the Gump is flying?' persisted the boy. 'We cannot see a single thing down on the earth, and before morning we may be far beyond the place we want to reach.'

'That is all true enough,' the Scarecrow replied a little uneasily. 'But I do not see how we can stop just now; for we might alight in a river, or on the top of a steeple, and that would be a great disaster.'

So they permitted the Gump to fly on, with regular flops of its great wings, and waited for morning.

Then Tip's fears proved to be well founded; for with the first streaks of grey dawn they looked over the sides of the sofas and discovered rolling plains dotted with queer villages, where the houses, instead of being dome-shaped —as they all are in the Land of Oz—had slanting roofs that rose to a peak in the centre. Odd-looking animals were also moving about upon the open plains, and the country was unfamiliar to both the Tin Woodman and the Scarecrow, who had formerly visited Glinda the Good's domain and knew it well.

'We are lost!' said the Scarecrow, dolefully. 'The Gump must have carried us entirely out of the Land of Oz and over the sandy deserts and into the terrible outside world that Dorothy told us about.'

'We must get back,' exclaimed the Tin Woodman earnestly; 'we must get back as soon as possible!'

'Turn around!' cried Tip to the Gump. 'Turn as quickly as you can!'

'If I do, I shall upset,' answered the Gump. 'I'm not at all used to flying, so the best plan would be for me to alight in some place, and then I can turn around and take a fresh start.'

At that moment, however, there seemed to be no stopping place that would answer their purpose. They flew over a village so big that the Wogglebug declared it was a city. Then they came to a range of high mountains with many deep gorges and steep cliffs.

'Now is our chance to stop,' said the boy, finding they were very close to the mountaintops. Then he turned to the Gump and commanded, 'Stop at the first level place you see!'

'Very well,' answered the Gump. He flew down to settle on a table of rock between two cliffs.

But he was not experienced in such matters and did not judge his speed correctly; instead of coming to a stop on the flat rock, he missed it by half the width of his sofa-body. He broke off both his right wings against the sharp edge of the rock and tumbled over and over down the cliff.

Our friends held on to the sofas as long as they could; but when the Gump caught on a projecting rock, he stopped suddenly—bottom side up—and all his passengers were dumped out.

By good fortune they fell only a few feet, for underneath them was a monster nest, built by a colony of Jackdaws in a hollow ledge of rock; so none of them—not even the Pumpkinhead—was injured by the fall. For Jack found his precious head resting on the soft breast of the Scarecrow, which made an excellent cushion; and Tip fell on a mass of leaves and papers, which saved him from injury. The Wogglebug had bumped his round head against the Sawhorse, but he was not hurt.

The Tin Woodman was at first much alarmed; but finding he had escaped without even a scratch upon his beautiful nickel-plate, he at once regained his accustomed cheerfulness and turned to address his comrades.

'Our journey has ended rather suddenly,' said he, 'and we cannot justly blame our friend the Gump for our accident, because he did the best he could. But how are we ever to escape from this nest? I must leave that to someone with better brains than mine.'

Here he gazed at the Scarecrow, who crawled to the edge of the nest and looked over. Below them was a sheer precipice several hundred feet in depth. Above them was a smooth cliff, unbroken save by the point of rock where the wrecked Gump still hung suspended. There really seemed no way to escape.

'This is a worse prison than the palace,' sadly remarked the Wogglebug.

'I wish we had stayed there,' moaned Jack. 'I'm afraid the mountain air isn't good for pumpkins.'

'It won't be when the Jackdaws come back,' growled the Sawhorse, which lay waving its legs in a vain endeavour to get upon its feet again. 'Jackdaws are especially fond of pumpkins.'

'Do you think the birds will come here?' asked Jack, much distressed.

'Of course they will,' said Tip, 'for this is their nest. And there must be hundreds of them,' he continued, 'for see what a lot of things they have stolen.'

Indeed the nest was half-filled with a most curious collection of small articles for which the birds could have no use. The Jackdaws had stolen them from the homes of men during many years of thieving. And as their nest was safely hidden where no human being could reach it, the lost property would never be recovered.

The Wogglebug, searching among the rubbish—for the Jackdaws stole useless things as well as valuable ones— turned up with his foot a beautiful diamond necklace. This was so greatly admired by the Tin Woodman that the Wogglebug presented it to him with a graceful speech, after which the Woodman hung it around his neck with much pride, rejoicing exceedingly when the big diamonds glittered in the sun's rays.

But now they heard a great jabbering and flopping of wings, and as the sound came nearer Tip exclaimed, 'The Jackdaws are coming! And if they find us here they will surely kill us in their anger.'

'I was afraid of this!' moaned the Pumpkinhead. 'My time has come!'

'And mine also,' said the Wogglebug, 'for Jackdaws are the greatest enemies of my race!'

The others were not at all afraid, but the Scarecrow at once decided to save those of the party who were liable to be injured by the angry birds. So he commanded Tip to take off Jack's head and lie down with it in the bottom of the nest, and when this was done he ordered the Wogglebug to lie beside Tip. Nick Chopper, who knew from past experience just what to do then took out the Scarecrow's stuffing—all except his head—and scattered the straw over Tip and the Wogglebug, completely covering them.

Hardly had this been accomplished when the flock of Jackdaws reached them. Seeing the intruders in their nest, the birds flew down upon them with screams of rage.

19.

Dr. Nikidik's Famous Wishing Pills

THE TIN WOODMAN was usually a peaceful man, but when occasion required he could fight as fiercely as a Roman gladiator. So when the Jackdaws nearly knocked him down in their rush of wings, and their sharp beaks and claws threatened to damage his brilliant plating, the Woodman picked up his axe and made it whirl swiftly around his head.

Many Jackdaws were beaten off, but the birds were so numerous and brave that they continued to attack furiously. Some of them pecked at the eyes of the Gump, which hung over the nest in a helpless condition; but the Gump's eyes were of glass and could not be injured. Others of the Jackdaws rushed at the Sawhorse; but that animal, being still upon his back, kicked out so viciously with his wooden legs that he beat off as many assailants as did the Woodman's axe.

Finding themselves thus opposed, the birds fell upon the Scarecrow's straw, which lay at the centre of the nest, covering Tip and the Wogglebug and Jack's pumpkin head, and began tearing it away and flying off with it, only

to let it drop, straw by straw into the great gulf beneath.

The Scarecrow's head, noting with dismay this wanton destruction of his vital stuffing, cried to the Tin Woodman to save him; and that good friend responded with renewed energy. His axe fairly flashed among the Jackdaws, and fortunately the Gump began wildly waving the two wings remaining on the left side of its body. The flutter of these great wings filled the Jackdaws with terror; and when the Gump, by its exertions, freed itself from the peg of rock on which it hung and sank flopping into the nest, the alarm of the birds knew no bounds and they fled screaming over the mountains.

When the last foe had disappeared, Tip crawled from under the sofas and assisted the Wogglebug to follow him.

'We are saved!' shouted the boy delightedly.

'We are indeed!' responded the educated insect, fairly hugging the stiff head of the Gump in his joy; 'and we owe it all to the flopping of the Gump and the good axe of the Woodman!'

'If I am saved, get me out of here!' called Jack, whose head was still beneath the sofas; and Tip managed to roll the pumpkin out and place it on its neck again. He also set the Sawhorse upright, and said, 'We owe you many thanks for your gallant fight.'

'I really think we have escaped very nicely,' remarked the Tin Woodman, in a tone of pride.

'Not so!' exclaimed a hollow voice.

At this they all turned in surprise to look at the Scarecrow's head, which lay at the back of the nest.

'I am completely ruined!' declared the Scarecrow, as

he noted their astonishment. 'For where is the straw that stuffs my body?'

The awful question startled them all. They gazed around the nest with horror, for not a vestige of straw remained. The Jackdaws had stolen it to the last wisp and flung it all into the chasm that yawned for hundreds of feet beneath the nest.

'My poor, poor friend!' said the Tin Woodman, taking up the Scarecrow's head and caressing it tenderly. 'Whoever could imagine you would come to this untimely end?'

'I did it to save my friends,' returned the head; 'and I am glad that I perished in so noble and unselfish a manner.'

'But why are you all so despondent?' inquired the Wogglebug: 'The Scarecrow's clothing is still safe.'

'Yes,' answered the Tin Woodman, 'but our friend's clothes are useless without stuffing.'

'Why not stuff him with money?' asked Tip.

'Money!' they all cried, in an amazed chorus.

'To be sure,' said the boy. 'In the bottom of the nest are thousands of dollar bills—and two-dollar bills—and five-dollar bills—and tens, and twenties, and fifties. There are enough of them to stuff a dozen scarecrows. Why not use the money?'

The Tin Woodman began to turn over the rubbish with the handle of his axe; and sure enough, what they had first thought only worthless papers were found to be dollar bills of various denominations, which the mischievous Jackdaws had, over the years, been stealing from the villages and cities they visited.

There was an immense fortune lying in that nest; and with the Scarecrow's consent, Tip's suggestion was quickly acted upon.

The selected all the newest and cleanest bills and sorted them into various piles. The Scarecrow's left leg and boot were stuffed with five-dollar bills, his right leg was stuffed with ten-dollar bills, and his body so closely filled with fifty-, one-hundred-, and one-thousand-dollar bills that he could scarcely button his jacket.

'You are now,' said the Wogglebug impressively, when the task had been completed, 'the most valuable member of our party. But as you are among faithful friends, there is little danger of your being spent.'

'Thank you,' returned the Scarecrow gratefully. 'I feel like a new man; and although at first glance I might be mistaken for a safety deposit vault, I beg you to remember that my brains are still composed of the same old material. And these are the possessions that have always made me a person to be depended upon in an emergency.'

'Well, the emergency is here,' observed Tip; 'and unless your brains help us out of it, we shall pass the rest of our lives in this nest.'

'How about these Wishing Pills?' inquired the Scarecrow, taking the box from his jacket pocket. 'Can't we use them to escape?'

'Not unless we can count to seventeen by twos,' answered the Tin Woodman. 'But as our friend the Wogglebug claims to be highly educated, he should be able to figure out how that can be done.'

'It isn't a question of education,' returned the insect;

'it's merely a question of mathematics. I've seen the Professor work lots of sums on the blackboard, and he claimed anything could be done with x's and y's and a's, and such things, by mixing them up with plenty of plusses and minuses and equals, and so forth. But he never said anything, as far as I can remember, about counting up to the odd number of seventeen by twos.'

'Stop! Stop!' cried the Pumpkinhead. 'You're making my head ache.'

'And mine,' added the Scarecrow. 'Your mathematics seems to me like a bottle of mixed pickles—the more you fish for what you want, the less chance you have of getting it. I am certain that if the thing can be accomplished at all, it can be done very simply.'

'Yes,' said Tip; 'old Mombi couldn't use x's and minuses, for she never went to school.'

'Why not start counting at a half of one?' asked the Sawhorse abruptly. 'Then anyone can count up to seventeen by twos very easily.'

They looked at each other in surprise, for the Sawhorse was considered the most stupid of the entire party.

'You make me quite ashamed of myself,' said the Scarecrow, bowing low to the Sawhorse.

'Nevertheless, the creature is right,' declared the Wogglebug; 'for twice one half is one, and if you get to one it is easy to count from one up to seventeen by twos.'

'I wonder I didn't think of that myself,' said the Pumpkinhead.

'I don't' returned the Scarecrow. 'You're no wiser than the rest of us, are you? But let us make a wish at once. Who will swallow the first pill?'

'Suppose you do it,' suggested Tip.

'I can't,' said the Scarecrow.

'Why not? You've a mouth, haven't you?'

'Yes; but my mouth is painted on, and there's no swallow connected with it,' answered the Scarecrow. 'In fact,' he continued, looking from one to another critically, 'I believe the boy and the Wogglebug are the only ones in our party that are able to swallow.'

Observing the truth of this remark, Tip said:

'Then I will undertake to make the first wish. Give me one of the silver pills.'

This the Scarecrow tried to do; but his padded gloves were too clumsy to clutch so small an object, and he held the box towards the boy while Tip selected one of the pills and swallowed it.

'Count!' cried the Scarecrow.

'One half, one, three, five, seven, nine, eleven, thirteen, fifteen, seventeen!' counted Tip.

'Now wish!' said the Tin Woodman anxiously.

But just then the boy began to suffer such fearful pains that he became alarmed.

'The pill has poisoned me!' he gasped; 'O—h! O-o-o-o-o! Ouch! Murder! Fire! O-o-h!' and here he rolled upon the bottom of the nest in such contortions that he frightened them all.

'What can we do for you? Speak, I beg!' entreated the Tin Woodman, tears of sympathy running down his nickel cheeks.

'I—I don't know!' answered Tip. 'O—h! I wish I'd

never swallowed that pill!'

Then at once the pain stopped, and the boy rose to his feet again and found the Scarecrow looking with amazement in the bottom of the pepper-box.

'What's happened?' asked the boy, a little ashamed of his recent exhibition.

'Why, the three pills are in the box again!' said the Scarecrow.

'Of course they are,' the Wogglebug declared. 'Didn't Tip wish that he'd never swallowed one of them? Well, the wish came true, and he *didn't* swallow one of them. So of course they are all three in the box.'

'That may be; but the pill gave me a dreadful pain, just the same,' said the boy.

'Impossible!' declared the Wogglebug. 'If you have never swallowed it, the pill can not have given you a pain. And as your wish, being granted, proves you did not swallow the pill, it is also plain that you suffered no pain.'

'Then it was a splendid imitation of a pain,' retorted Tip angrily. 'Suppose you try the next pill yourself. We've wasted one wish already.'

'Oh no, we haven't!' protested the Scarecrow. 'Here are still three pills in the box, and each pill is good for a wish.'

'Now you're making *my* head ache,' said Tip. 'I can't understand the thing at all. But I won't take another pill, I promise you!' and with this remark he retired sulkily to the back of the nest.

'Well,' said the Wogglebug, 'it remains for me to save us in my most Highly Magnified and Thoroughly Educated manner, for I seem to be the only one able and willing to make a wish. Let me have one of the pills.'

He swallowed it without hesitation, and they all stood admiring his courage while the insect counted seventeen by twos in the same way that Tip had done. And for some reason—perhaps because Wogglebugs have stronger stomachs than boys—the silver pellet caused it no pain whatever.

'I wish the Gump's broken wings mended and as good as new!' said the Wogglebug in a slow, impressive voice.

All turned to look at the Gump, and so quickly had the wish been granted that the thing lay before them in perfect repair, and as well able to fly through the air as when it had first been brought to life on the roof of the palace.

20.

The Scarecrow Appeals to Glinda

'HOORAY!' shouted the Scarecrow gaily. 'We can now leave this miserable Jackdaws' nest whenever we please.'

'But it is nearly dark,' said the Tin Woodman; 'and unless we wait until morning to make our flight, we may get into more trouble. I don't like these night trips, for one never knows what will happen.'

So it was decided to wait until daylight, and the adventurers amused themselves in the twilight by searching the Jackdaws' nest for treasures.

The Wogglebug found two handsome bracelets of wrought gold, which fitted his slender arms very well. The Scarecrow took a fancy to rings, of which there were many in the nest. Before long he had fitted a ring to each finger of his padded gloves, and not being content with that display he added one more to each thumb. As he carefully chose those rings set with sparkling stones, such as rubies, amethysts, and sapphires, the Scarecrow's hands now presented a most brilliant appearance.

'This nest would be a picnic for Queen Jinjur,' said he musingly; 'for as nearly as I can make out, she and her girls conquered me merely to rob my city of its emeralds.'

The Tin Woodman was content with his diamond necklace, and refused to accept any additional decorations; but Tip secured a fine gold watch, which was attached to a heavy fob, and placed it in his pocket with much pride. He also pinned several jewelled brooches to Jack Pumpkinhead's pink waistcoat, and attached a lorgnette, by means of a fine chain, to the neck of the Sawhorse.

'It's very pretty,' said the creature, regarding the lorgnette approvingly, 'but what is it for?'

None of them could answer that question, however, so the Sawhorse decided it was some rare decoration and became very fond of it.

That none of the party might be slighted, they ended by placing several large seal rings upon the points of the Gump's antlers.

Darkness soon fell; while Tip and the Wogglebug went to sleep, the others sat down to wait patiently for dawn.

Next morning they had reason to be glad of the Gump's useful condition, for with daylight a great flock of Jackdaws swooped down to battle again for possession of their nest.

But our adventurers did not wait for the assault. They tumbled quickly into the cushioned seats of the sofas, and Tip told the Gump to start.

At once it rose into the air, the great wings flopping strongly, and in a few moments they were far from the nest. The Jackdaws did not attempt to pursue them.

They flew due north, flying always in the same direction they had come from. After passing over several cities and villages, the Gump carried them high above a broad plain, where the houses were more and more scattered until they disappeared altogether. Next came the wide, sandy desert separating the rest of the world from the Land of Oz, and before noon they saw the dome-shaped houses that proved they were once more within the borders of their native land.

'But the houses and fences are blue,' said the Tin Woodman, 'and that indicates we are in the land of the Munchkins, and therefore a long distance from Glinda the Good.'

'What shall we do?' asked the boy, turning to their guide.

'I don't know,' replied the Scarecrow, frankly. 'If we were at the Emerald City we could then move directly southward, and so reach our destination. But we dare not go to the Emerald City, and the Gump is probably carrying us farther in the wrong direction with every flop of its wings.'

'Then the Wogglebug must swallow another pill,' said Tip decidedly, 'and wish us headed in the right direction.'

'Very well,' returned the highly magnified one; 'I'm willing.'

But when the Scarecrow searched in his pocket for the pepper-box containing the two silver Wishing Pills, it could not be found. Filled with anxiety, the voyagers searched every inch of the thing for the precious box, but it had disappeared entirely.

And still the Gump flew onward, carrying them they knew not where.

'I must have left the pepper-box in the Jackdaws' nest,'

said the Scarecrow at length.

'It is a great misfortune,' the Tin Woodman declared. 'But we are no worse off than before we discovered the Wishing Pills.'

'We are better off,' replied Tip, 'for with the one pill we were able to escape from that horrible nest.'

'Yet the loss of the other two is serious, and I deserve a good scolding for my carelessness,' the Scarecrow rejoined penitently. 'For in such an unusual party as this, accidents are liable to happen any moment. Even now we may be approaching a new danger.'

No one dared contradict this, and a dismal silence ensued.

The Gump flew steadily on.

Suddenly Tip uttered an exclamation of surprise.

'We must have reached the South Country,' he cried, 'for below us everything is red!'

Immediately they all leaned over the backs of the sofas to look—all except Jack, who was too careful of his pumpkin head to risk its slipping off his neck. Sure enough: the red houses and fences and trees indicated they were within the domain of Glinda the Good; and presently, as they glided rapidly on, the Tin Woodman recognized the roads and buildings they passed, and altered the Gump's direction slightly to make sure they reached the palace of the celebrated Sorceress.

'Good!' cried the Scarecrow delightedly. 'We do not need the lost Wishing Pills now, for we have arrived at our destination.'

Gradually the thing sank lower and nearer to the

ground, until it came to rest within the beautiful gardens
of Glinda. It settled upon a velvety lawn close by a foun-
tain which sent sprays of flashing gems, instead of water,
high into the air.

Everything was very gorgeous in Glinda's gardens; and
while our voyagers gazed about with admiring eyes, a
company of soldiers silently appeared and surrounded
them. But these soldiers of the great Sorceress were entirely different from those of Jinjur's Army of Revolt, although they also were girls. For Glinda's soldiers wore
neat uniforms and bore swords and spears, and they
marched with a skill and precision that proved them well
trained in the arts of war.

The Captain commanding this troop, which was
Glinda's private Body Guard, recognized the Scarecrow
and the Tin Woodman at once, and greeted them with
respectful salutations.

'Good day!' said the Scarecrow, gallantly removing his
hat, while the Woodman gave a soldierly salute. 'We have
come to request an audience with your fair ruler.'

'Glinda is now within her palace, awaiting you,' returned the Captain, 'for she saw you coming long before
you arrived.'

'That is strange!' said Tip, wondering.

'Not at all,' answered the Scarecrow, 'Glinda the Good
is a mighty Sorceress, and nothing that goes on in the Land
of Oz escapes her notice. I suppose she knows why we
came as well as we do ourselves.'

'Then what's the use of our coming?' asked Jack.

'To prove you are a Pumpkinhead!' retorted the Scarecrow. 'But if the Sorceress expects us, we must not keep her waiting.'

So they all climbed out of the sofas and followed the Captain toward the palace; even the Sawhorse took his place in the queer procession.

Upon her throne of finely wrought gold sat Glinda, and she could scarcely repress a smile as her odd visitors entered and bowed before her. Both the Scarecrow and the Tin Woodman she knew and liked; but the awkward Pumpkinhead and Highly Magnified Wogglebug were creatures she had never seen before, and they seemed even more curious than the others. As for the Sawhorse, he looked to be nothing more than an animated chunk of wood; and he bowed so stiffly that his head bumped against the floor, causing a ripple of laughter among the soldiers, in which Glinda frankly joined.

'I beg to announce to Your Glorious Highness,' began the Scarecrow in a solemn voice, 'that my Emerald City has been overrun by a crowd of impudent girls with knitting needles, who have enslaved all the men, robbed the streets and public buildings of all their emerald jewels, and usurped my throne.'

'I know it,' said Glinda.

'They also threatened to destroy me, as well as all the good friends and allies you see before you,' continued the Scarecrow; 'and had we not managed to escape their clutches, our days would long have ended.'

'I know it,' repeated Glinda.

'Therefore I have come to beg your assistance,' resumed the Scarecrow, 'for I believe you are always glad to succour the unfortunate and oppressed.'

'That is true,' replied the Sorceress slowly. 'But the Emerald City is now ruled by General Jinjur, who has caused herself to be proclaimed Queen. What right have I to oppose her?'

'Why, she stole the throne from me,' said the Scarecrow.

'And how came you to possess the throne?' asked Glinda.

'I got it from the Wizard of Oz, and by the choice of the people,' returned the Scarecrow, uneasy at such questioning.

'And where did the Wizard get it?' she continued, gravely.

'I am told he took it from Pastoria, the former King,' said the Scarecrow, becoming confused under the intent look of the Sorceress.

'Then,' declared Glinda, 'the throne of the Emerald City belongs neither to you nor to Jinjur, but to this Pastoria from whom the Wizard usurped it.'

'That is true,' acknowledged the Scarecrow humbly; 'but Pastoria is now dead and gone, and someone must rule in his place.'

'Pastoria had a daughter, who is the rightful heir to the throne of the Emerald City. Did you know that?' questioned the Sorceress.

'No,' replied the Scarecrow. 'But if the girl still lives I will not stand in her way. It will satisfy me just as well to have Jinjur turned out as an impostor as to regain the throne myself. In fact, it isn't much fun to be King, especially if one has good brains. I have known for some time that I am fitted to occupy a far more exalted position. But where is this girl who owns the throne, and what is her name?'

'Her name is Ozma,' answered Glinda. 'But where she is I have tried in vain to discover. For the Wizard of Oz, when he stole the throne from Ozma's father, hid the girl in some secret place; and by means of a magical trick with which I am not familiar he also managed to prevent her being discovered—even by so experienced a Sorceress as myself.'

'That is strange,' interrupted the Wogglebug, pompously. 'I have been informed that the Wonderful Wizard of Oz was nothing more than a humbug!'

'Nonsense!' exclaimed the Scarecrow, much provoked by this speech. 'Didn't he give me a wonderful set of brains?'

'There's no humbug about my heart,' announced the Tin Woodman, glaring at the Wogglebug.

'Perhaps I was misinformed,' stammered the insect, shrinking back; 'I never knew the Wizard personally.'

'Well, we did,' retorted the Scarecrow, 'and he was a very great Wizard, I assure you. It is true he was guilty of some slight impostures, but unless he was a great Wizard, how—let me ask—could he have hidden this girl Ozma so securely that no no can find her?'

'I—I give it up!' replied the Wogglebug meekly.

'That is the most sensible speech you've made,' said the Tin Woodman.

'I must really make another effort to discover where this girl is hidden,' resumed the Sorceress thoughtfully. 'I have in my library a book in which is inscribed every action of the Wizard while he was in our Land of Oz—or at least every action that could be observed by my spies. This book I will read carefully tonight, and try to single out the acts that may guide us in discovering the lost Ozma. In the meantime, pray amuse yourselves in my palace and command my servants as if they were your own. I will grant you another audience tomorrow.'

With this gracious speech Glinda dismissed the adventurers, and they wandered away through the beautiful gardens, where they passed several hours enjoying all the delightful things with which the Queen of the Southland had surrounded her royal palace.

On the following morning they again went to talk with Glinda the Good. She said to them:

'I have searched carefully through the records of the Wizard's actions, and among them I can find but three that appear to have been suspicious. He ate beans with a knife, made three secret visits to old Mombi, and limped slightly on his left foot.'

'Ah! That last is certainly suspicious!' exclaimed the Pumpkinhead.

'Not necessarily,' said the Scarecrow; he may have had corns. Now it seems to me his eating beans with a knife is more suspicious.'

'Perhaps it is a polite custom in Omaha, from which great country the Wizard originally came,' suggested the Tin Woodman.

'It may be,' admitted the Scarecrow.

'But why,' asked Glinda, 'did he make three secret visits

to old Mombi?'

'Ah! Why, indeed!' echoed the Wogglebug.

'We know that the Wizard taught the old woman many of his tricks of magic,' continued Glinda, 'and this he would not have done had she not assisted him in some way. So we may suspect with good reason that Mombi aided him to hide the girl Ozma, who was the real heir to the throne of the Emerald City, and a constant danger to the usurper. For if the people knew that she lived, they would quickly make her their Queen and restore her to her rightful position.'

'An able argument!' cried the Scarecrow. 'I have no doubt that Mombi was mixed up in this wicked business. But how does that knowledge help us?'

'We must find Mombi,' replied Glinda, 'and force her to tell where the girl is hidden.'

'Mombi is now with Queen Jinjur in the Emerald City,' said Tip. 'It was she who threw so many obstacles in our pathway, and made Jinjur threaten to destroy my friends

and get me back in her power.'

'Then,' decided Glinda, 'I will march with my army to the Emerald City and take Mombi prisoner. After that we can perhaps force her to tell the truth about Ozma.'

'She is a terrible old woman!' remarked Tip, with a shudder at the thought of Mombi's black kettle. 'And obstinate, too.'

'I am quite obstinate myself,' returned the Sorceress, with a sweet smile, 'so I do not fear Mombi in the least. To-day I will make all necessary preparations, and we will march upon the Emerald City at daybreak tomorrow.'

21.

The Tin Woodman Plucks a Rose

THE ARMY OF GLINDA THE GOOD looked very grand and imposing when it assembled at daybreak before the palace gates. The uniforms of the girl soldiers were pretty and of gay colours, and their silver-tipped spears were bright and glistening, the long shafts being inlaid with mother-of-pearl. All the officers wore sharp, gleaming swords, and shields edged with peacock feathers; and it really seemed that no foe could by any possibility defeat such a brilliant army.

The Scarecrow and his comrades decided to ride in the Gump, in order to keep up with the swift march of the army; so as soon as Glinda had started and her soldiers had marched away to the inspiring strains of music played by the royal band, our friends climbed into the sofas and followed. The Gump flew along slowly at a point directly over the palanquin in which rode the Sorceress.

'Be careful,' said the Tin Woodman to the Scarecrow, who was leaning far over the side to look at the army below. 'You might fall.'

'It wouldn't matter,' remarked the educated Wogglebug; 'he can't be broke as long as he is stuffed with money.'

'Didn't I ask you——' began Tip.

'You did!' said the Wogglebug, promptly. 'And I beg your pardon. I will really try to restrain myself.'

'You'd better,' declared the boy. 'That is, if you wish to travel in our company.'

'Ah! I couldn't bear to part with you now,' murmured the insect feelingly; so Tip let the subject drop.

The army moved steadily on, but night had fallen before they came to the walls of the Emerald City. By the dim light of the new moon, however, Glinda's forces silently surrounded the city and pitched their tents of scarlet silk upon the greensward. The tent of the Sorceress was larger than the others, and was composed of pure white silk, with scarlet banners flying above it. A tent was also pitched for the Scarecrow's party; and when these preparations had been made, with military precision and quickness, the army retired to rest.

Great was the amazement of Queen Jinjur next morning when her soldiers came running to inform her of the vast army surrounding them. She at once climbed to a high tower of the royal palace and saw banners waving in every direction, and the great white tent of Glinda standing directly before the gates.

'We are surely lost!' cried Jinjur in despair. 'For how can our knitting needles avail against the long spears and terrible swords of our foes?'

'The best thing we can do,' said one of the girls, 'is to surrender quickly before we get hurt.'

'No so,' returned Jinjur, more bravely. 'The enemy is

still outside the walls, so we must try to gain time by engaging them in parley. Go you with a flag of truce to Glinda and ask her why she has dared to invade my dominions, and what are her demands.'

So the girl passed through the gates, bearing a white flag to show she was on a mission of peace, and came to Glinda's tent.

'Tell your Queen,' said the Sorceress to the girl, 'that she must deliver up to me old Mombi, to be my prisoner. If this is done I will not trouble her farther.'

Now when this message was delivered to the Queen it filled her with dismay; for Mombi was her chief counsellor, and Jinjur was terribly afraid of the old hag. But she sent for Mombi, and told her what Glinda had said.

'I see trouble ahead for all of us,' muttered the old Witch, after glancing into a magic mirror she carried in her pocket. 'But we may even yet escape by deceiving this Sorceress, clever as she thinks herself.'

'Don't you think it will be safer for me to deliver you into her hands?' asked Jinjur, nervously.

'If you do, it will cost you the throne of the Emerald City!' answered the Witch positively. 'But if you will let me have my own way, I can save us both.'

'Then do as you please,' replied Jinjur, 'for it is so aristocratic to be a Queen that I do not wish to return home to make beds and wash dishes for my mother.'

So Mombi called Jellia Jamb to her and performed a certain magical rite with which she was familiar. As a result of the enchantment, Jellia took on the form and features of Mombi, while the old Witch grew to resemble the girl so closely that it seemed impossible anyone could guess the deception.

'Now,' said old Mombi to the Queen, 'let your soldiers deliver up this girl to Glinda. She will think she has the real Mombi in her power, and so will return immediately to her own country in the South.'

Therefore Jellia, hobbling along like an aged woman, was led from the city gates to Glinda.

'Here is the person you demanded,' said one of the guards, 'and our Queen now begs you will go away, as you promised, and leave us in peace.'

'That I will surely do,' replied Glinda, much pleased, 'if this is really the person she seems to be.'

'It is certainly old Mombi,' said the guard, who believed she was speaking the truth; and then Jinjur's soldiers returned within the city's gates.

The Sorceress quickly summoned the Scarecrow and his friends to her tent and began to question the supposed Mombi about the lost girl Ozma. But Jellia knew nothing at all of this affair, and presently she grew so nervous under the questioning that she gave way and began to weep!

'Here is some foolish trickery!' said the Sorceress, her eyes flashing with anger. 'This is not Mombi at all, but some other person who has been made to resemble her! Tell me,' she demanded, turning to the trembling girl, 'what is your name?'

This Jellia dared not tell, having been threatened with death by the Witch if she confessed the fraud. But Glinda, sweet and fair though she was, understood magic better

than any other person in the Land of Oz. So, by uttering a
few potent words and making a peculiar gesture, she
quickly transformed the girl into her proper shape, while
at the same time old Mombi, far away in Jinjur's palace,
suddenly resumed her own crooked form and evil features.

'Why, it's Jellia Jamb!' cried the Scarecrow, recogniz-
ing in the girl one of his old friends.

'It's our interpreter!' said the Pumpkinhead.

Then Jellia was forced to tell of the trick Mombi had
played, and she also begged Glinda's protection, which
the Sorceress readily granted. But Glinda was now really
angry, and sent word to Jinjur that the fraud was discovered and she must deliver up the real Mombi or suffer
terrible consequences. Jinjur was prepared for this message, for the Witch well understood, when her natural
form was thrust upon her, that Glinda had discovered her
trickery. But the wicked old creature had already thought
up a new deception, so Jinjur said to Glinda's messenger:

'Tell your mistress that I cannot find Mombi anywhere,
but that Glinda is welcome to enter the city and search
herself for the old woman. She may also bring her friends
with her, if she likes; but if she does not find Mombi by
sundown, the Sorceress must promise to go away peace-
ably and bother us no more.'

Glinda agreed to these terms, well knowing that Mombi
was somewhere within the city walls. So Jinjur caused the
gates to be thrown open, and Glinda marched in at the
head of a company of soldiers, followed by the Scarecrow
and the Tin Woodman, while Jack Pumpkinhead rode
astride the Sawhorse.

Of course old Mombi had no intention of being found by Glinda, so while her enemies were marching up the street, the Witch transformed herself into a red rose growing upon a bush in the garden of the palace. It was a clever idea, and a trick Glinda did not suspect; so several precious hours were spent in a vain search for Mombi.

As sundown approached, the Sorceress realized she had been defeated by the superior cunning of the aged Witch; so she gave the command to her people to march out of the city and back to their tents.

The Scarecrow and his comrades happened to be searching in the garden of the palace just then, and they turned with disappointment to obey Glinda's command. But before they left the garden, the Tin Woodman, who was fond of flowers, chanced to espy a big red rose growing upon a bush; so he plucked the flower and put it in his buttonhole.

As he did this, he fancied he heard a low moan proceed from the rose; but he paid no attention to the sound, and Mombi was thus carried out of the city and into Glinda's camp without anyone knowing it.

22.

The Transformation of Old Mombi

THE WITCH WAS AT FIRST FRIGHTENED at finding herself captured by the enemy, but soon she decided that she was exactly as safe in the Tin Woodman's buttonhole as growing upon the bush. For no one knew the rose and Mombi to be one; and now that she was without the gates of the city, her chances of escaping altogether from Glinda were much improved.

'But there is no hurry,' thought Mombi. 'I will wait a while and enjoy the humiliation of this Sorceress when she finds I have outwitted her.'

So throughout the night the rose lay quietly on the Woodman's bosom; and in the morning, when Glinda summoned our friends to a consultation, Nick Chopper carried his pretty flower with him to the white silk tent.

'For some reason,' said Glinda, 'we have failed to find this cunning old Mombi, so I fear our expedition will prove a failure. And for that I am sorry, because without our assistance little Ozma will never be rescued and restored to her rightful position as Queen of the Emerald City.'

'Do not let us give up so easily,' said the Pumpkinhead. 'Let us do something else.'

'Something else must really be done,' replied Glinda with a smile; 'yet I cannot understand how I have been defeated so easily by an old Witch who knows far less of magic than I do myself.'

'While we are on the ground I believe it would be wise for us to conquer the Emerald City for Princess Ozma, and find the girl afterwards,' said the Scarecrow. 'And while the girl remains hidden I will gladly rule in her place, for I understand the business of ruling much better than Jinjur does.'

'But I have promised not to molest Jinjur,' objected Glinda.

'Suppose you all return with me to my kingdom—or empire, rather,' said the Tin Woodman, politely including the entire party in a royal wave of his arm. 'It will give me great pleasure to entertain you in my castle, where there is room enough and to spare. And if any of you wish to be nickel-plated, my valet will do it free of all expense.'

While the Woodman was speaking, Glinda's eyes had been noting the rose in his buttonhole and now she imagined she saw the big red leaves of the flower tremble slightly. This quickly aroused her suspicions, and in a moment more the Sorceress had decided that the seeming rose was nothing else than a transformation of old Mombi. At the same instant Mombi knew she was discovered and must quickly plan an escape; and as transformations were easy to her, she immediately took the form of a shadow and glided along the wall of the tent towards the entrance, thinking thus to disappear.

But Glinda had not only equal cunning but far more experience than the Witch. So the Sorceress reached the opening of the tent before the shadow, and with a wave of her hand closed the entrance so securely that Mombi could not find a crack big enough to creep through. The Scarecrow and his friends were greatly suprised at Glinda's actions, for none of them had noted the shadow. But the Sorceress said to them:

'Remain perfectly quiet, all of you! For the old Witch is even now with us in this tent, and I hope to capture her.'

These words so alarmed Mombi that she quickly transformed herself from a shadow to a black ant, in which shape she crawled along the ground, seeking a crack or crevice in which to hide her tiny body.

Fortunately, the ground where the tent had been pitched, being just before the city gates, was hard and smooth; and while the ant still crawled about, Glinda discovered it and ran quickly forward to effect its capture. But just as her hand was descending, the Witch, now fairly frantic with fear, made her last transformation, and in the form of a huge Griffin sprang through the wall of the tent —tearing the silk asunder in her rush—and in a moment had darted away with the speed of a whirlwind.

Glinda did not hesitate to follow: She sprang upon the back of the Sawhorse and cried:

'Now you shall prove that you have a right to be alive! Run—run—run!'

The Sawhorse ran. Like a flash he followed the Griffin, his wooden legs moving so fast that they twinkled like the rays of a star. Before our friends could recover from their surprise both the Griffin and the Sawhorse had dashed out of sight.

'Come! Let us follow!' cried the Scarecrow.

They ran to the place where the Gump was lying, and quickly tumbled aboard.

'Fly!' commanded Tip eagerly.

'Where to?' asked the Gump in its calm voice.

'I don't know,' returned Tip, who was very nervous at the delay; 'but if you will mount into the air, I think we can discover which way Glinda has gone.'

'Very well,' returned the Gump quietly, and it spread its great wings and mounted high into the air.

Far away, across the meadows, they could now see two tiny specks, speeding one after the other; and they knew these specks must be the Griffin and the Sawhorse. So Tip called the Gump's attention to them and bade the creature try to overtake the Witch and the Sorceress. But swift as was the Gump's flight, the pursued and pursuer moved more swiftly yet, and within a few moments were blotted out against the dim horizon.

'Let us continue to follow them, nevertheless,' said the Scarecrow; 'for the Land of Oz is of small extent, and sooner or later they must both come to a halt.'

Old Mombi had thought herself very wise to choose the form of a Griffin, for its legs were exceedingly fleet, and its strength more enduring than that of other animals. But she had not reckoned on the untiring energy of the Sawhorse, whose wooden limbs could run for days without slacking their speed. Therefore, after an hour's hard running, the Griffin's breath began to fail, and it panted and gasped painfully, and moved more slowly than before. Then it reached the edge of the desert and began racing across the deep sands. But its tired feet sank far into the sand, and in a few minutes the Griffin fell forward, completely exhausted, and lay still upon the desert waste.

Glinda came up a moment later, riding the still vigorous Sawhorse; and having unwound a slender golden thread from her girdle the Sorceress threw it over the head of the panting and helpless Griffin, and so destroyed the magical power of Mombi's transformation.

For the animal, with one fierce shudder, disappeared from view, while in its place was discovered the form of the old Witch, glaring savagely at the serene and beautiful face of the Sorceress.

23.

Princess Ozma
of Oz

'YOU ARE MY PRISONER, and it is useless for you to struggle
any longer,' said Glinda, in her soft, sweet voice. 'Lie still
a moment and rest yourself, and then I will carry you back
to my tent.'

'Why do you seek me?' asked Mombi, still scarce able
to speak plainly for lack of breath. 'What have I done to
you, to be so persecuted?'

'You have done nothing to me,' answered the gentle
Sorceress, 'but I suspect you have been guilty of several
wicked actions; and if I find it is true that you have so
abused your knowledge of magic, I intend to punish you
severely.'

'I defy you!' croaked the old hag. 'You dare not harm
me!'

Just then the Gump flew up to them and alighted upon
the desert sands beside Glinda. Our friends were delighted
to find that Mombi had finally been captured, and after
a hurried consultation it was decided they should all return to the camp in the Gump. So the Sawhorse was tossed
aboard, and then Glinda, still holding an end of the golden

thread that was around Mombi's neck, forced her prisoner
to climb into the sofas. The others now followed, and Tip
gave the word to the Gump to return.

The journey was made in safety, Mombi sitting in her
place with a grim and sullen air; for the old hag was abso-
lutely helpless as long as the magical thread encircled her
throat. The army hailed Glinda's return with loud cheers,
and the party of friends soon gathered again in the royal
tent, which had been neatly repaired during their absence.

'Now,' said the Sorceress to Mombi, 'I want you to tell
us why the Wonderful Wizard of Oz paid you three visits,
and what became of the child Ozma, which so curiously
disappeared.'

The Witch looked at Glinda defiantly, but said not a
word.

'Answer me!' cried the Sorceress.

But still Mombi remained silent.

'Perhaps she doesn't know,' remarked Jack.

'I beg you will keep quiet,' said Tip. 'You might spoil
everything with your foolishness.'

'Very well, dear Father!' returned the Pumpkinhead
meekly.

'How glad I am to be a Wogglebug!' murmured the
highly magnified insect softly. 'No one can expect wisdom
to flow from a pumpkin.'

'Well,' said the Scarecrow, 'what shall we do to make
Mombi speak? Unless she tells us what we wish to know,
her capture will do us no good at all.'

'Suppose we try kindness,' suggested the Tin Woodman.
'I've heard that anyone can be conquered with kindness,

no matter how ugly he may be.'

At this the Witch turned to glare upon him so horribly that the Tin Woodman shrank back abashed.

Glinda had been carefully considering what to do, and now she turned to Mombi and said:

'You will gain nothing, I assure you, by thus defying us. For I am determined to learn the truth about the girl Ozma, and unless you tell me all that you know, I will certainly put you to death.'

'Oh no! Don't do that!' exclaimed the Tin Woodman. 'It would be an awful thing to kill anyone—even old Mombi!'

'But it is merely a threat,' returned Glinda. 'I shall not put Mombi to death, because she will prefer to tell me the truth.'

'Oh, I see!' said the Tin Woodman, much relieved.

'Suppose I tell you all that you wish to know,' said Mombi, speaking so suddenly that she startled them all. 'What will you do with me then?'

'In that case,' replied Glinda, 'I shall merely ask you to drink a powerful draught which will cause you to forget all the magic you have ever learned.'

'Then I would become a helpless old woman!'

'But you would be alive,' suggested the Pumpkinhead consolingly.

'Do try to keep silent!' said Tip nervously.

'I'll try,' responded Jack; 'but you will admit that it's a good thing to be alive.'

'Especially if one happens to be Thoroughly Educated,' added the Wogglebug, nodding approval.

'You may make your choice,' Glinda said to old Mombi, 'between death—if you remain silent—and the loss of your magical powers—if you tell me the truth. But I think you will prefer to live.'

Mombi cast an uneasy glance at the Sorceress, and saw that she was in earnest and not to be trifled with. So she replied, slowly:

'I will answer your questions.'

'That is what I expected,' said Glinda pleasantly. 'You have chosen wisely, I assure you.'

She then motioned to one of her captains, who brought her a beautiful golden casket. From this the Sorceress drew an immense white pearl attached to a slender chain, which she placed around her neck in such a way that the pearl rested upon her bosom, directly over her heart.

'Now,' said she, 'I will ask my first question: Why did the Wizard pay you three visits?'

'Because I would not come to him,' answered Mombi.

'That is no answer,' said Glinda sternly. 'Tell me the truth.'

'Well,' returned Mombi, with downcast eyes, 'he visited me to learn the way I make tea biscuits.'

'Look up!' commanded the Sorceress.

Mombi obeyed.

'What is the colour of my pearl?' demanded Glinda.

'Why—it is black!' said the old Witch.

'Then you have told me a falsehood!' cried Glinda angrily. 'Only when the truth is spoken will my magic pearl remain a pure white in colour.'

Mombi now saw how useless it was to try to deceive the

Sorceress, so she said, meanwhile scowling at her defeat:

'The Wizard brought to me the girl Ozma, who was then no more than a baby, and begged me to conceal the child.'

'That is what I thought,' declared Glinda calmly. 'What did he give you for thus serving him?'

'He taught me all the magical tricks he knew. Some were good tricks, and some were only frauds; but I have remained faithful to my promise.'

'What did you do with the girl?' asked Glinda; and at this question everyone bent forward and listened eagerly for the reply.

'I enchanted her,' answered Mombi.

'In what way?'

'I transformed her into—into—'

'Into what?' demanded Glinda.

'*Into a boy!*' said Mombi, in a low tone.

'A boy!' echoed every voice; and then, because they knew that this old woman had reared Tip from childhood, all eyes were turned to the boy.

'Yes,' said the old Witch, nodding her head; 'that is the Princess Ozma—the child brought to me by the Wizard who stole her father's throne. That is the rightful ruler of the Emerald City!' and she pointed her long bony finger straight at the boy.

'I!' cried Tip in amazement. 'Why, I'm no Princess Ozma—I'm not a girl!'

Glinda smiled, and going to Tip she took his small brown hand within her dainty white one.

'You are not a girl just now,' said she gently, 'because

Mombi transformed you into a boy. But you were born a
girl, and also a Princess; so you must resume your proper
form, that you may become Queen of the Emerald City.'

'Oh, let Jinjur be the Queen!' exclaimed Tip, ready to
cry. 'I want to stay a boy, and travel with the Scarecrow
and the Tin Woodman, and the Wogglebug, and Jack—
yes! and my friend the Sawhorse—and the Gump! I
don't want to be a girl!'

'Never mind, old chap,' said the Tin Woodman soothingly; 'it doesn't hurt to be a girl, I'm told; and we will

all remain your faithful friends just the same. And, to be honest with you, I've always considered girls nicer than boys.'

'They're just as nice, anyway,' added the Scarecrow, patting Tip affectionately upon the head.

'And they are equally good students,' proclaimed the Wogglebug. 'I should like to become your tutor, when you are transformed into a girl again.'

'But—see here!' said Jack Pumpkinhead, with a gasp. 'You won't be my dear Father any more!'

'No,' answered Tip, laughing in spite of his anxiety; 'and I shall not be sorry to escape the relationship.' Then he added, hesitatingly, as he turned to Glinda : 'I might try it for a while—just to see how it seems, you know. But if I don't like being a girl, you must promise to change me into a boy again.'

'Really,' said the Sorceress, 'that is beyond my magic. I never deal in transformations, for they are not honest, and no respectable Sorceress likes to make things appear to be what they are not. Only unscrupulous Witches use the art, and therefore I must ask Mombi to effect your release from her charm and restore you to your proper form. It will be the last opportunity she will have to practise magic.'

Now that the truth about the Princess Ozma had been discovered, Mombi did not care what became of Tip; but she feared Glinda's anger, and the boy generously promised to provide for Mombi in her old age if he became the ruler of the Emerald City. So the Witch consented to effect the transformation, and preparations for the event were made at once.

Glinda ordered her own royal couch to be placed in the centre of the tent. It was piled high with cushions covered with rose-coloured silk, and from a golden railing above hung many folds of pink gossamer, completely concealing the interior of the couch.

The first act of the Witch was to make the boy drink a potion, which quickly sent him into a deep and dreamless sleep. Then the Tin Woodman and the Wogglebug bore him gently to the couch, placed him upon the soft cushions, and drew the gossamer hangings to shut him from all earthly view.

The Witch squatted upon the ground and kindled a tiny fire of dried herbs, which she drew from her bosom. When the blaze shot up and burned clearly, old Mombi scattered a handful of magical powder over the fire, which straightway gave off a rich violet vapour, filling all the tent with its fragrance and forcing the Sawhorse to sneeze —although he had been warned to keep quiet.

Then, while the others watched her curiously, the hag chanted a rhythmical verse in words which no one understood, and bent her lean body seven times back and forth over the fire. And now the incantation seemed complete, for the Witch stood upright and cried the one word 'Yeowa!' in a loud voice.

The vapour floated away; the atmosphere became clear again; a whiff of fresh air filled the tent, and the pink curtains of the couch trembled slightly, as if stirred from within.

Glinda walked to the canopy and parted the silken

hangings. Then she bent over the cushions, reached out her hand, and from the couch arose the form of a young girl, fresh and beautiful as a May morning. Her eyes sparkled as two diamonds, and her lips were the colour of rubies. Down her back flowed her golden hair, and she wore a slender jewelled circlet on her brow. Her robes of silk floated around her like a cloud, and on her feet were dainty slippers.

At this exquisite vision Tip's old comrades stared in wonder for a full minute, and then every head bent low in admiration of the lovely Princess Ozma. The girl herself cast one look into Glinda's bright face, which glowed with pleasure and satisfaction, and then turned to the others. Speaking the words with sweet diffidence, she said:

'I hope none of you will care less for me than you did before. I'm just the same Tip, you know; only——'

'Only you're different!' said the Pumpkinhead; and everyone thought it was the wisest speech he had ever made.

24.
The Riches of Content

WHEN THE WONDERFUL TIDINGS reached the ears of Queen Jinjur—how Mombi the Witch had been captured, how she had confessed her crime to Glinda, and how the long-lost Princess Ozma had been discovered in no less a personage than the boy Tip—she wept real tears of grief and despair.

'To think,' she moaned, 'that after having ruled as Queen and lived in a palace, I must go back to scrubbing floors and churning butter again! It's too awful!'

So when her soldiers, who spent most of their time making fudge in the palace kitchens, counselled Jinjur to resist, she listened to their foolish prattle and sent a sharp defiance to Glinda the Good and the Princess Ozma. The result was a declaration of war, and the very next day Glinda marched upon the Emerald City with pennants flying and bands playing, and a forest of shining spears sparkling brightly beneath the sun's rays.

But when it came to the walls, this brave assembly made a sudden halt; for Jinjur had closed and barred every gateway, and the walls of the Emerald City were built high and thick with many blocks of green marble. Finding her advance thus baffled, Glinda bent her brows in deep thought, while the Wogglebug said, in his most positive tone:

'We must lay siege to the city and starve it into submission. It is the only thing we can do.'

'Not so,' answered the Scarecrow. 'We still have the Gump, and the Gump can still fly.'

The Sorceress turned quickly at this speech, and her face now wore a bright smile.

'You are right,' she exclaimed, 'and you certainly have reason to be proud of your brains. Let us go to the Gump at once!'

So they passed through the ranks of the army until they came to the place, near the Scarecrow's tent, where the Gump lay. Glinda and Princess Ozma mounted first, and sat upon the sofas. Then the Scarecrow and his friends climbed aboard, and still there was room for a captain and three soldiers, which Glinda considered sufficient for a guard.

Now, at a word from the Princess, the queer Gump flopped its palm-leaf wings and rose into the air, carrying the party of adventurers high above the walls. They hovered over the palace, and soon perceived Jinjur reclining in a hammock in the courtyard, where she was comfortably reading a novel with a green cover and eating green chocolates, confident that the walls would protect her from her enemies. Obeying a quick command, the Gump alighted safely in this very courtyard; and before Jinjur had time to do more than scream, the captain and three

soldiers leaped out and made the former Queen a prisoner, locking strong chains upon both her wrists.

That act really ended the war; for the Army of Revolt submitted as soon as they knew Jinjur to be a captive, and the captain marched in safety through the streets and up to the gates of the city, which she threw wide open. Then the bands played their most stirring music while Glinda's army marched into the city, and heralds proclaimed the conquest of the audacious Jinjur and the accession of the beautiful Princess Ozma to the throne of her royal ancestors.

At once the men of the Emerald City cast off their aprons. And it is said that the women were so tired of eating of their husbands' cooking that they all hailed the conquest of Jinjur with joy. Certain it is that, rushing one and all to the kitchens of their houses, the good wives prepared so delicious a feast for the weary men that harmony was immediately restored.

Ozma's first act was to oblige the Army of Revolt to return to her every emerald or other gem stolen from the public streets and buildings, and so great was the number of precious stones picked from their settings by these vain girls that every one of the royal jewellers worked steadily for more than a month to replace them in their settings.

Meantime the Army of Revolt was disbanded and the girls sent home to their mothers. On promise of good behaviour, Jinjur was likewise released.

Ozma made the loveliest Queen the Emerald City had ever known, and although she was so young and inexperienced, she ruled her people with wisdom and justice. For Glinda gave her good advice on all occasions; and the Wogglebug, who was appointed to the important post of Public Educator, was quite helpful to Ozma when her royal duties grew perplexing.

The girl, in her gratitude to the Gump for its services, offered the creature any reward it might name.

'Then,' replied the Gump, 'please take me to pieces. I did not wish to be brought to life, and I am greatly ashamed of my conglomerate personality. Once I was a monarch of the forest, as my antlers fully prove; but now, in my present upholstered condition of servitude, I am compelled to fly through the air—my legs being of no use to me whatever. Therefore I beg to be dispersed.'

So Ozma ordered the Gump taken apart. The antlered

head was again hung over the mantelpiece in the hall, and the sofas were untied and placed in the reception parlours. The broom tail resumed its accustomed duties in the kitchen, and finally the Scarecrow replaced all the clothes-lines and ropes on the pegs from which he had taken them on the eventful day when the thing was constructed.

You might think that was the end of the Gump—and so it was, as a flying machine. But the head over the mantel-piece continued to talk whenever it took a notion to do so; and it frequently startled, with its abrupt questions, the people who waited in the hall for an audience with the Queen.

The Sawhorse, being Ozma's personal property, was tenderly cared for; and often she rode the queer creature along the streets of the Emerald City. She had its wooden legs shod with gold, to keep them from wearing out, and the tinkle of these golden shoes upon the pavement always filled the Queen's subjects with awe as they thought upon this evidence of her magical powers.

'The Wonderful Wizard was never so wonderful as Queen Ozma,' the people said to one another in whispers; 'for he claimed to do many things he could not do, whereas our new Queen does many things no one would ever expect her to accomplish.'

Jack Pumpkinhead remained with Ozma to the end of his days; and he did not spoil as soon as he had feared, although he always remained as stupid as ever. The Woggle-bug tried to teach him several arts and sciences; but Jack was so poor a student that any attempt to educate him was soon abandoned.

After Glinda's army had marched back home, and peace was restored to the Emerald City, the Tin Woodman announced his intention to return to his own Kingdom of the Winkies.

'It isn't a very big kingdom,' said he to Ozma, 'but for that very reason it is easier to rule; and I have called myself Emperor because I am an absolute Monarch, and no one interferes in any way with my conduct of public or personal affairs. When I get home I shall have a new coat of nickel-plate, for I have become somewhat marred and scratched lately; and then I shall be glad to have you pay me a visit.'

'Thank you,' replied Ozma. 'Someday I may accept the invitation. But what is to become of the Scarecrow?'

'I shall return with my friend the Tin Woodman,' said the stuffed one seriously. 'We have decided never to be parted in the future.'

'And I have made the Scarecrow my Royal Treasurer,' explained the Tin Woodman. 'For it has occurred to me that it is a good thing to have a Royal Treasurer who is made of money. What do you think?'

'I think,' said the little Queen, smiling, 'that your friend must be the richest man in all the world.'

'I am,' returned the Scarecrow, 'but not on account of my money. For I consider brains far superior to money, in every way. You may have noticed that if one has money without brains, he cannot use it to advantage; but if one has brains without money, they will enable him to live comfortably to the end of his days.'

'At the same time,' declared the Tin Woodman, 'you

must acknowledge that a good heart is a thing that brains cannot create and that money cannot buy. Perhaps, after all, it is I who am the richest man in all the world.'

'You are both rich, my friends,' said Ozma gently, 'and your riches are the only riches worth having—the riches of content!'

The following Classics are also
available in Armada

By Louis M. Alcott
Little Women
Good Wives

By Lewis Caroll
Alice in Wonderland

By Susan M. Coolidge
What Katy Did
What Katy Did At School
What Katy Did Next

By Anthony Hope
Rupert of Hentzau
The Prisoner of Zenda

By Thomas Hughes
Tom Brown's Schooldays

By Anna Sewell
Black Beauty

By Joanna Spyri
Heidi

By R. L. Stevenson
Treasure Island
Kidnapped

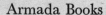

Armada Books

They are wonderful, with their gay spines adding colour to your bookshelf. Are you collecting your own library of Armada books? A book a week . . . or a month . . . and in no time you would have a marvellous collection! *Start today!* Always ask your bookseller or newsagent for Armada books, but if you have difficulty in getting the titles you want write to Armada Books, 14 St. James's Place, London, S.W.1. Overseas readers should write to the same address for information about their nearest stockists, etc.

BOOKS AVAILABLE INCLUDE

Mystery and Adventure Stories by

Ruth M. Arthur   Captain W. E. Johns
Enid Blyton   Carolyn Keene
Richmal Crompton   Malcolm Saville
Alfred Hitchcock

School Stories by

Angela Brazil   Anthony Buckeridge
Elinor M. Brent-Dyer   Frank Richards

Pony and Animal Stories by

Judith M. Berrisford   Hazel M. Peel
Monica Edwards   Martha Robinson
Mary Gervaise   M. E. Patchett
The Pullein-Thompson sisters

AND MANY OTHERS, including some Classics

For current stock list please send a stamped self-addressed envelope to Armada Books, 14 St. James's Place, London S.W.1.